THE SERPENT OF WOODLANDS

Garth Green

ISBN-13: 9798592841200
ISBN-10: 147712340

Cover design by: Garth Green
Preface by: Darryl Wilbur
Photograph by: Roman Iwasiwka
Library of Congress Control Number: 2018675309
Printed in the United States of America

For

My Mother, who read to me as a child,
which entertained and inspired me.

My Father, who's love of the fine arts
endowed me with the same appreciation.

My Brother, who picked on me when I was little,
I give thanks for preparing me for the world.

To Sarah, who gave me her love.

PREFACE

Garth Green sets his semi-biographical story around his first job on a large, distinguished estate full of natural beauty. He takes the name Flint, an exceptional guitar player with the idealistic dream to become a famous musician. Flint and the estate owner's beautiful daughter, Julie, fall in love, both for the first time. Julie, however, is in danger of being kidnapped by a malevolent shape-shifting frog-like creature who is also in love with her. The author creatively sprinkles the suspenseful plot with a gallant serpent and a few supernatural characters who support and protect Julie against this danger. Readers will become nostalgic remembering their first cars, loves, jobs, and dreams. In the epilogue to this story, Flint returns to the estate 40 years later and the strong emotion the reader feels upon learning the eventual fates of the story's characters is a testimony to the author's skill in creating characters to which the reader becomes attached.

THE SERPENT OF WOODLANDS

1

The year was 1982, and the sun was slowly setting on a beautiful, warm summer afternoon in the countryside of England. Nestled in small patch of forest fifteen miles outside of Wiltshire resided the Clark family. A father, his daughter, a house maid, a dog, and a cat all shared a small cottage estate named Pine Manor. On that relaxing, picturesque day everything was calm and normal, but exciting, life-changing events were soon to unfold for this small and loving family.

There was a slight breeze in the air, and the afternoon shadows were now stretching across the grounds. Dividing the garden from the cottage was a tall stone wall covered with mature, thick ivy. From the cottage's open windows came the sound of a well-performed rendition of Rachmaninoff's 3rd concerto, played masterfully on a baby grand piano by the owner, Ethan Clark.

While Ethan continued to play, a five-year-old large, white Pyrenees dog lay beside the piano. Ethan's loyal dog King loved to listen to him play while napping on living room floor.

King was given to Ethan as a wedding gift from his boyhood friend, Ian. King loved Ethan, and ever since he was a puppy, he was faithful to Ethan's well-being and safety.

Ethan Clark was of average height, a good-looking man with a chiseled face and wavy, reddish-blonde hair combed behind his ears. For the past seventeen years he taught senior high school English and directed the drama club. Well-liked by students for his youthful approach to teaching, Ethan would also get their adoration and attention by animating the characters in the books they were studying.

Ethan and his wife Sarah of eighteen years had inherited the Pine Manor estate from Sarah's father, Joseph Cooper, a wealthy man who made his money in the early 1920's from the sale of sewing thread.

Mr. Cooper's daughter Sarah was a beautiful, wholesome, and intelligent woman whose interests included gardening, animals, and politics. Two years ago, Sarah became ill with cancer and abruptly passed, leaving Ethan to handle the estate and care for their only daughter, Julie. Deeply distraught by the loss, Ethan felt the need for a change and made plans to move the United States so Julie could study fashion design in New York City.

On the other side of the living room eighteen-year-old Julie stood frantically drawing pictures of women posing with various accessories such as pocketbooks and umbrellas.

Julie's figure was slender and shapely. She had a round face with long black, corkscrew hair and high cheekbones that revealed two little dimples in her checks when she smiled. Julie also had a deep appreciation for nature like her mother, but her desire was to become a fashion designer. She would make faces while drawing, going back and forth from a pinched, irritated look to a warm smile that revealed her two whimsical dimples.

Outside the living quarters atop the ten-foot stone wall lay the family cat, Polly. She was a small gray cat with a tiny tip of white on her tail and a thin line of white between her eyes.

Polly was seven years old, but her stature was that of an adolescent cat. Nonetheless, she had the smarts, agility, and hunting skills of a Bengal tiger. Polly lay contently on the garden wall while shifting her gaze to both sides. She too was enjoying the piano music but was also keeping a watchful eye on the garden below. Polly always eagerly awaited a lazy vole or perhaps something of an altogether different nature.

It was at that moment there were just such beings carefully tucked under the fattest poppy plant in the garden, a pair of fairies named Foster and Faye. Both sat enjoying the warm summer air, as they listened Ethan's piano playing.

The fairies were the secret and unseen caretakers of Pine Manor. They were both well over one hundred years of age but barely showed it. Neither of them sported wings for they were ground workers in the fairy kingdom.

Foster and Faye had originally worked with other fairies on the well-known Finn horn Gardens in England. Though many of their co-workers had left to escape the pollution and ignorance of the humankind, Foster and Faye decided to continue their existence in this realm with Ethan's family. They were especially fond of Sarah since she was so well acquainted with all the plantings and flowers grown in the garden.

Foster sported a jet-black beard along with long hair tied in a ponytail. He had a kind face with deep, enigmatic blue eyes and wore a pair of overalls. His talents were many, but he had a weakness for the milk of the poppy.

Faye had long, dark brown hair that she wore in two braids on either side. Her almond-shaped emerald green eyes were prominent above a thin, small reddish nose. She wore a long-sleeve turtleneck, underneath a tight purple vest, and preferred to wear pants rather than a dress.

Both fairies complimented each other well and they had boundless energy, despite their age. Their powers to aid in the growth of plants and flowers had been cultivated from the masters they worked alongside, but their talents were soon to be put to an entirely different challenge.

Ethan had just finished the concerto, and he remained seated before the piano. Despite his blessings, the forthcoming decision to move to another country weighed heavy on his mind.

After several moments of quiet contemplation, he began to improvise on a composition which he had begun earlier. The soothing melodies were brilliantly executed with quick and fluent motion from his nimble fingers. As he fervently expressed his inner emotions with his own composition, Foster and Faye listened intently.

Faye quietly stated to Foster, "I love to listen to Ethan play the famous composers' works; he executes them with such precision."

Foster replied, "Yes, but I prefer his own compositions. I find the human spirit vibrates on an entirely different level when invoking one's own deep feelings, very much like when we are assisting the flowers' growth instead of just tending to the soil."

Faye nodded her head slowly, "Yes, I understand what you say, but it does seem his loss is still fresh in his heart, and it worries me to see him still so melancholy. Perhaps it's a good thing they are moving to the states. Ethan needs to separate himself from the memories of Sarah. However, I'm going to miss this place very much, and I'm not so sure it's a wise decision to leave."

Foster grabbed her by the hand, "We have done some great work here, but as you know everything changes and I believe it's time to start a new chapter."

Faye slightly closed her eyes and slowly nodded in acceptance. "I genuinely love the earth and all its beauty and don't wish to move on like the other fairies have. When does Ethan plan on leaving?"

Foster looked upward. "I believe all of us are leaving by ocean liner next weekend. We should go now and prepare for the transition. Dear me! Polly has spotted us, so we best make our exit now."

Just at that moment Julie's voice called for Polly. Since there weren't any voles or mice to be found in the garden, her stomach welcomed some canned tuna instead. Like an arrow released from a bow, Polly sped to the back door of the cottage. Once inside, she made a beeline to her feeding bowl.

Meanwhile, Nadia, the family's house maid, was masterfully preparing a roast pork for the family in the kitchen. Nadia was of Lithuanian decent, but her English was particularly good thanks to Ethan's coaching. She was thirty-five, a tall woman with dark black hair wrapped in a loose beehive atop her head.

Nadia also liked to splash on plenty of perfume and had a rather large bust that she would show off by wearing tight, thin sweaters. Nadia was a caring person who always made sure the family and their pets were well attended to.

Evening was ending on the estate. The lights were bright inside the dining room with everyone sitting at the table engaging in conversation about their day. King sat under the table with his tail wagging, anticipating multiple table scraps from Ethan. Polly decided to remain curled in her wicker basket keeping a watchful eye on it all.

Julie asked, "Father, could you tell us more about this place in the states we are moving to?"

He replied, "Well... it's called The Woodlands Estate, and it's located sixty miles north of New York City. It is a total of eighty-one acres. There are multiple buildings throughout the property: a gatehouse, cabin, main house, bath house, barn, green house, and plenty of forest, hence the name Woodlands. It may be a bit more property than we need, but it comes with a permanent gardener along with a small crew presently involved in the construction of a new bath house. There are even some chickens and a couple of goats. The grounds are well-maintained, and there is a large pond with a walkway that connects to a three-season, hexagonal gazebo."

Julie exclaimed with an exciting tone in her voice, "This all sounds very wonderful and intriguing."

Nadia elatedly replied, "This place sounds great; I am so thankful that you have arranged for me to join you." In her excitement Nadia's voice became louder as she turned to Julie, "So close to New York City with all the stores and culture. I am extremely excited! Aren't you Julie?"

Julie looked back at her with a big smile. "Of course, I am, but there are so many memories of this place and mother. I also feel a bit nervous about the big city. I'm such a nature girl."

Sensing Julie's reluctance, Ethan replied, "You will have the best of both worlds, plenty of trees and only a half hour from the city. In two more weeks, we'll all be crossing the Atlantic bound for the states. Julie, your mother will always be with us no matter where we are. I honestly believe this."

Nadia raised her glass of wine and joyfully exclaimed, "I'll drink to that and America."

Dinner was then followed by some evening news on the television and some delicious homemade ice cream.

Back in the kitchen King and Polly lay together contently full of leftover table scraps. They were also enjoying the warm breeze from the nearby open window.

Both animals were able to communicate between themselves but never engaged with their ability to speak to the humans.

King looked over at Polly and cocked his head, "What's going on in that furry, feline brain of yours?"

Polly replied, "Well for one thing I'm not looking forward to this boat trip. We'll be almost two weeks floating in water, and I'm not very fond of even the thought of getting wet."

King replied, "Stop being so fussy. You'll be thrilled once we get there. I heard there will be three times more land to hunt – why never a dull moment!"

Polly stopped licking one of her paws. "Well, I just don't want to go. Why do we always have to do what Ethan wants all the time?"

King gave her a stern stare and replied, "Now I know you're more independent than me, but I would go anywhere with him. After all, he saved me when I was only a year old from the frozen pond in the back of the house."

King proceeded to recollect the event. "The ice cracked, and I fell in, frantically paddling to stay above the water. There was no way I could escape until Ethan and his friend Ian pulled me out using a nearby broken branch."

King then turned his head looking down to the left. "At the same time the water became very green and something else beneath the water pushed me up. It was strange how it all happened so fast. Ethan is my savior, and I'll never forget that day for the rest of my life."

Polly's tail twitched and replied, "I know you're right. He is a particularly good master. Julie is such a sweet and caring guardian as well. I would miss curling up to her warm belly every night. Do you know if Faye and Foster are coming too?"

King nodded, "Of course! I heard them planning on how they are going to stow away in the baby grand piano."

Polly raised her head from a curled position, "Really? Those two certainly are adventurous!"

King flattened himself onto the floor and then raised his head to Polly, "Now I'm full and very tired. If you don't mind, could you leave me to rest awhile?"

Polly stood on all fours and gave King a blank stare. "Alright, King. I feel the same, but first I'm going to see if there are any empty ice cream bowls to lick clean."

2

T he following weeks flew by as all the preparations were made for the family's departure from Pine Manor. The day had finally come to embark on their new life. It was agreed between them to travel by ocean liner so they could be close to their pets and experience travel the old-fashioned way many Europeans had traveled decades ago.

All three were standing together on the ship. Ethan, decked out in a sharp British suit, lifted his head, and opened his eyes wide. "Well, are you two prepared to brave the high seas and salty air?"

Julie replied, "Guess so father, but I feel we are leaving important people, things and memories behind."

"Perhaps Julie, but we've all had to process much in the past two years, and we can still stay in touch with our friends here."

Julie nodded to her father but was quickly distracted when for an instant she saw something swiftly skimming the surface of the water. It was followed by a bright green flash as it quickly disappeared. Perplexed momentarily, her attention was then shifted back to the dock by a joyful shout that came from Ethan's friend, Ian.

Ian stood on the dock waving his hands shouting, "Bon Voyage! Don't forget to write. Love you guys!"

Ian and Ethan shared many boyhood adventures and memories. He was a tall man who had the heart of a saint and a forever Peter Pan attitude. Ian put his imagination to good use and had become a well-known comic-book writer.

Ethan, Julie, and Nadia returned smiles and waved goodbye. The large ship slowly departed from the pier towards the horizon. Ian remained on the pier, still smiling, and waving.

Inside the ship King sat in a large blanket-filled cage wagging his tail as drool dripped from his half-open mouth. Polly sat curled in a ball inside her cage absolutely despising the whole ordeal.

A week into the trip everyone was enjoying themselves and finding the journey delightful. The voyage provided good weather and many memorable sunsets.

King and Polly had no complaints since they were given daily kitchen scraps, plenty of sweet talk and long petting intervals by Julie and several members of the crew.

Meanwhile Faye and Foster had just risen from their nap inside the baby grand piano. Faye had lined one of the chambers with plenty of soft blankets and pillows. Foster had collected a nice assortment of dried fruits, grapes, and a small jar of poppy milk to aid them in sleeping through majority of the trip.

Faye turned and asked Foster, "Are you alright dear?

Wake up, sleepy brain. I'm hungry!"

Slowly arising Foster mumbled, "Me too, let's eat." He shook the jar of fireflies and slowly a dim glow of light was cast across both their faces.

After they finished their smorgasbord of goodies, Foster took Faye's hand and squeezed it hard. "You know, before we woke up, I was having a very strange dream."

Faye gave him a long stare. "Well, we have plenty of time to kill so go ahead and tell me everything about this dream you had."

Foster gazed straight ahead, reflecting on his dream, and continued. "Remember that time we were looking for wild blueberries on the mountain overlooking the pond?"

Faye nodded, "Oh yes, and we both saw that long wiggly thing in the water at the north end. Yes, I remember, and we were trying to figure out what the hell it was."

Foster continued, "In my dream I was walking into the pond until I was fully underwater. I remember feeling relaxed with a sense of peace and I was also able to breath under water. Suddenly, dead ahead of me was this smiling face slowly coming closer and closer. At first, all I could see was a pair of eyes. Then a creature with fins and a long body came face to face with me. It just stopped and smiled at me. The creature then started to speak, but then I woke up."

Faye stared back. "Interesting, but I'm sure the milk of the poppy had much to do with this dream; don't you think?"

"Perhaps, Faye, but it felt and looked so real. I really think that the creature was trying to communicate something important to me."

Faye tilted her head to acknowledge interest. "Alright, maybe so, but I need to stretch my legs. Let's go for a walk."

◆ ◆ ◆

On the other end of the ship in the captain's quarters the First Mate, Geoffrey, and Captain Scott were recapping the journey's highlights so far. Both were delighted that they didn't encounter any severe weather on the voyage.

First mate Geoffrey looked the Captain in the eye, cleared his throat and said, "Off the record here Captain, but just before we left England, I noticed something long in the water moving fast alongside the vessel."

The Captain had a doubtful look in his face as he raised his eyebrow and said, "Really? What do you think it was?"

With a wide-eyed expression the First mate replied, "Well, I thought it was a squid, but they usually don't come that close to shore. Then it disappeared the moment I locked eyes on it. I flicked on the sonar to see if it would appear on the screen, but I saw absolutely nothing. I chalked it up to being a reflection in the water from a passing speed boat leaving the dock."

The Captain rolled his eyes to the ceiling, "Yes, it was probably just that."

"But wait a second Captain. Before I came to your quarters, I checked the screen again and something did show. It was a rather long object moving amazingly fast, but then it vanished."

"Alright Geo I'm not doubting you saw something, but we're almost to port, and I really don't want to log this incident in the journal."

"Aye, Captain Scott, understood. I just had to let someone know about it. I agree, best to forget the whole thing. However, it was a rather colorful and curious thing."

3

I t was a hot and humid Monday morning when the large station wagon followed by a long moving truck approached the entrance to the Woodlands Estate. Turning right into the driveway entrance, everyone was enamored by the tall trees that towered over the road. Old stone walls covered in dried moss lined the drive. Beyond them were dense clusters of pachysandras followed by mature rhododendron bushes that we're practically the size of small trees.

Further ahead on the left stood the gatehouse. This structure was slightly reminiscent of a Swiss chalet. The driveway continued straight ahead, and the tree canopy grew taller, blocking out much of the morning sunlight. It was three quarters of a mile to the main house, and already everyone found the first introduction to Woodlands quite enchanting.

Still tucked away inside the baby grand piano, Foster and

Faye were stiff and very much ready to touch the earth again.

"Enough of this piano! Cozy as it may be, I've had it," said Faye.

In a groggy voice Foster replied, "Yes, double that! I can't wait to see what this place looks like. I also hope Ethan has made a wise choice. He usually has a strong gut sense, but perhaps he was hoping only to satisfy Julie's interest."

The truck rolled along and passed an old stone cabin on the right. Up ahead there was an opening in the trees, and the light started to fill the car, causing everyone's eyes to squint.

The vehicles then drove over a small stone bridge that crossed over the north end of a large pond that expanded out to their right.

Just at that moment, Foster's eyes widened with a look of panic on his face.

Faye asked, "What in the world was that look?"

With a trance-like stare on his face, Foster replied, "I just felt an extraordinarily strong presence below this truck. Something not from this world and frighteningly negative I'm afraid."

"Really, that's not good." Faye replied.

◆ ◆ ◆

The station wagon and the moving van finally rolled in front of the main house. The driveway continued in a circle and then continued up a short hill. Tall oak trees towered around most of the circular portion of the driveway. Beneath them were more rhododendrons and laurel bushes.

The home looked to be built in the early nineteen thirties. It had pane glass windows on both floors and a wonderful large front porch. At the south end of the traffic circle was a tall cylindrical building with a  front door. It appeared to be a small farm silo. As the car stopped, all three simultaneously voiced, "Wow!"

Crouched on his knees opposite the front of the house was a gentleman next to a wheelbarrow. He was thin but muscular and wore a pair of dark green slacks and a V-neck white pocket tee with a pack of *Pall Mall* cigarettes stuffed in the pocket. He also had one of these non-filtered stogies hanging from the edge of his mouth.

This gentleman was named Mike, and he had been the gardener for the past fifteen years at the Woodlands Estate. He was a middle-aged Sicilian man with a chiseled jaw line, dark skin and piercing, dark brown eyes. His dark black hair was parted on the side with just a touch of gray on the temples.

Before the family arrived, he had been busy spreading bark mulch around the bases of the bushes. Now standing, he faced the new arrivals. He removed his gloves and then waved, giving everyone a warm smile.

Ethan stepped out of the station wagon and immediately locked eyes with Mike. He approached him while extending his hand and smiled, "Hello, I'm Ethan Clark the new owner."

Mike greeted Ethan and reciprocated with a firm handshake. "Nice to meet you, sir. Glad you made it here safely."

"Appreciate that, Mike. Come let me introduce you to everyone." Ethan turned and gestured to Julie and Nadia. "This is my daughter Julie and our wonderful cook and assistant Nadia."

Before any more conversation took place, King bounded out from the station wagon, wagging his tail, and smelling everyone and everything.

Poor Polly had to endure her cat carrier for another few moments until Julie excused herself and brought her into the house. Cats really don't show expression on their faces, but the urgency for a box was much needed.

Mike shook hands with Nadia and gave her a quick wink. "Welcome to Woodlands, and if you have any questions, feel free to ask."

Ethan glanced at the silo-like building. "Well, thanks, I do have one question. What is this small round building?"

With a serious look on his face Mike looked directly at Ethan. "That happens to be the original farm silo that was transformed into a children's playhouse. It was converted by the owner before the last."
Mike then focused his gaze to the treetops and continued. "Now I came here fifteen years ago, and the owner and his family had a young daughter, Emily. She was a cute little blonde-headed girl; she loved to spend hours in there. Except for an occasional cleaning nobody has been inside for a while now, but it's really rather magical in there." Mike looked to the ground now appearing somewhat melancholy. "Unfortunately, the girl only enjoyed it for a short spell being that she became ill and died from a blood disease. Poor thing was so cute and full of spunk. She utterly enjoyed that building. After all, she didn't have any brothers or sisters to play with." Mike abruptly changed his facial features and said, "Now let me help you with your belongings."

Ethan was bit sleepy and decided not to inquire any further and replied, "Well, thanks Mike, we have some movers to take care of the big items, but any help would be appreciated."

The main house didn't have much of a view from the east side, but facing west there was a picturesque view of the large pond below and the forest in the distance. A wonderful stone patio and a small patch of green lawn lined the back of the house. Lush beds of pachysandra covered the hill which was followed by more lawn that followed the entire length of the pond. At the far-left end of the pond, connected by a man-made earthen walkway, situated out in the water, was an octagonal screened in gazebo.

Nadia joined Julie inside the main house. Then they both ran up the stairs to have a look at the bedrooms.

Mike and Ethan then stepped out onto the back patio that overlooked the pond. Ethan was facing the pond while Mike was describing the history of the property to him.

Suddenly, from the corner of Ethan's sight, he thought he saw a large fish, or something come out of the water near the gazebo. It made a loud splash which made Mike halt his explanation, and they both turned to see what the noise was.

Ethan looked at Mike. "Guess you have some pretty big fish in this pond?"

Mike seemed somewhat mystified but replied, "Well no, not that I know of. It's only stocked with some carp that huddle near the gazebo, although there are some pretty big catfish in there."

Ethan, somewhat baffled, replied, "Well I only caught a glimpse of something; not sure what it was."

Mike answered, "It was probably a large branch falling out of one of the tall trees that border the pond. There's so much more to see. Allow me to continue the tour."

Ethan gave it no more thought and followed Mike through the rest of the house. After a brief walk-through they finally exiting the house from the basement.

They started walking on a blue-stone path that led downhill to a huge in-ground swimming pool that bordered a newly excavated clearing. Opposite the pool was the recently constructed Roman-style bath house.

The structure had six large columns that flanked the front. A series of multi-pane French doors with matching tall windows wrapped around the entire structure.

Inside the bath house were several workers, a handful of carpenters and three young men digging trenches for the water lines. Several different conversations and construction noise echoed inside as Ethan and Mike entered.

The tallest of the three diggers was a Scottish-looking young man named Ryan. He sported a full beard and a head of hair that resembled a wet, curly string mop. Ryan was the tallest and most well-build of the three. While during lunch breaks, he would often have plenty of colorful stories to tell about the folks from the jobs that he worked at before.

The fellow of middle height, Marco, was unmistakably Italian. He always wore a red bandanna and sported work boots with the laces untied. He was talking a mile a minute about one of his female conquests while playing air-guitar with his shovel. He was the clown of the bunch, and he always had a Cheshire cat-like grin plastered on his face.

The third youthful man, Flint, was no doubt the youngest. He was thin with long arms and had long brown hair that hung in front of his face. He was always trying to man up with the rest of the crew, but he was an artist – not a laborer.

Flint looked to be a cross between German and English descent and was no doubt not cut out for the type of work he was doing. He kept busy while listening to Marco's story and laughed at his antics.

Flint had left school in the eleventh grade in hopes of making it as a musician. His fantasies were dear to him, but realized he needed to earn money and manual labor was the only job that paid well.

Mike, the gardener, excused himself to Ethan and diverted his attention to Marco, still spinning his yarn. He rolled his eyes in his head and then called over to Flint, "Don't believe a single word of that story; he's full-of-it kid!"

Mike continued, "Say, guys, this is Mr. Clark the new owner of Woodlands. Now I want you to respect him, his family and especially his privacy – understand?"

They nodded hello to Ethan and then all responded in unison wearing big smiles on their faces. "Yes Mike!"

Mike turned to Ethan, "The carpenters and painters are hired to complete the bath house. The other three stooges are here to help me take care of the grounds. Mr. Clark, we have plenty of time to show you the rest. Why don't you go and get settled? I'll be around if you need me. It was nice meeting you. Good luck with the estate."

Ethan was looking forward to some down time and replied, "Thank you very much, Mike. I'm quite intrigued with the place already."

Later, the lunch hour arrived, and all three young men jumped in Ryan's car and took off downtown to the local deli.

Ryan turned on the car stereo, and a *Pink Floyd* song started playing. It was the part in the album *The Wall* where the helicopter blades are cutting through the air. Flint and the others listed intently as the thought entered each of their minds what it would be like on the battle-field. The helicopter noise reminded Flint of the recent movie *Apocalypse Now* and the terrors associated with combat.

The United States was unsure as to whether it was going to get involved with Iran and Iraq conflict. Registration had just been issued mandatory for the draft. The draft hadn't been issued since the Vietnam War, and up until now joining the service was only voluntary.

While downtown they picked up their sandwiches, and Marco grabbed a couple quarts of beer as well. Ryan hurried recklessly back to the estate to have more time for lunch. Ryan and Marco shouted curse words and flipped a couple middle fingers at slow-moving drivers as they passed them on the road. Flint just held on tight and enjoyed the music playing in the car.

Once they arrived, the three sat down by the bath house and devoured their sandwiches. They all complained how hot it was while they passed around the beer Marco bought.

Mike popped out of the corner of the property shaking his head with a smile. "Jesus, beer in the middle of the day? You kids are crazy drinking in this heat. You'll all be snoozing by three o'clock this afternoon."

Marco yelled back, "Aah lighten up, Mike, and have a swig!"

"Shit, why not." Mike replied. He then took a long slow gulp of the cold beer.

Mike finished and looked down at Flint. "Kid, they got you drinking this stuff too?"

"Yeah, Mike, it's so hot and my muscles are killing me." replied Flint.

"I know kid; it's alright. It sure is a hot one today. On top of that these black flies won't quit."

Ryan piped up, "Mike is there any bug repellent stashed in the greenhouse?"

"No, but what works for me is one of my extra-long *Pall Mall* cigarettes. Mike reached into his pocket; he passed a couple to Ryan and Marco. He turned to Flint with a blank stare and offered one to Flint and said, "Kid, even if you just keep it in your lips, the smoke will keep them little buggers off your face and head."

Flint never smoked a cigarette before, but he took one and replied, "I'll do anything to beat these nagging bugs. So sure – what the hell."

Everyone quickly fired up the non-filtered wonder stick and enjoyed the rest of the beer. Some mixed conversation continued about girls, cars and if they might be drafted.

It was now time to get back to work, and the little huddle broke up. Ryan and Marco headed for the bathroom, and Mike went back to spreading more mulch beneath the rhododendrons in front of the main house.

Standing alone next to the bath house, Flint was feeling a bit nauseous and light in the knees. The combination of the beer and cigarette made everything suddenly appear to be moving in slow motion. He needed to disappear, so he wandered off to the lawn next to the pond. Flint felt an overwhelming need to lay flat on his back and found a spot on the grass next to the water. The spins didn't stop, but he could cope much better than before.

Suddenly the sound of bugs and the rustling leaves coming from looming trees above became amplified. Flint was also aware of the sound of dripping water coming from the edge of the pond. His eyes were barely open when he felt a very definite presence behind him.

Flint stood up, turned around, wiped his eyes, and stepped back. At first all he could make out was what looked like the head of a horse. As his eyes focused, he saw a serpent-like creature covered in green scales, approximately seven feet in length. The creature had large expressive eyes with two horns protruding from the top of its head.

Flint was in utter awe of this unusual creature but despite his initial reaction, he felt calmer and more clear-headed than before.

To his amazement the creature started speaking in a mild-mannered British accent, "Do not be afraid my lad; I assure you, I am very real, and mean you no harm. My name is Martin. I saw that you needed some assistance, so I helped you gather your wits. Relax my boy and allow me to explain more about myself."

Martin took a deep breath and continued, "I have come a long way to be with this family from England. Many years ago, I was sent to your earth from another solar system to aid in their development. I have watched over Mr. Clark ever since he was a child. Like yourself, he is also a musician. He plays the piano whereas your passion is for the guitar; is this not so?"

Baffled how he knew this, Flint asked, "Why, yes, and how is it that you know I play guitar?"

Martin tilted his head slightly and momentarily gazed at Flint's hands. "Not only can I read your soul, but I see that your fingernails are longer on your right hand than your left. You use these fingernails to pluck the notes on your guitar, am I, not right?"

"Wow, yes! I'm amazed that not only can you read me, but that I'm actually talking to a serpent."

Martin blinked his eyes and continued. "Ethan and Julie's well-being are of my upmost importance and concern.

"And just how did you arrive here?" inquired Flint.

"As you can deduce, I'm not just your ordinary eel in the pond. Utilizing the unique energies of this earth, I am able to connect to any body of water on this planet."

"But wait a minute. I know they are not all connected. How is this possible?" Flint asked.

It is complicated and there is much to explain. That time will come, but for now, you need to rejoin your co-workers. I ask that you remain quiet about our meeting. For even Ethan and Julie are unaware of my existence. You and I have more to discuss but not currently.

Martin could sense that Flint was becoming overloaded. Now realizing it was time to leave, he closed by saying, "There is another reason I have contacted you. There's another entity that shares this pond, and unfortunately, he's not as friendly as me. We will have this discussion again when I find out more about him. Until then keep your ears and eyes open." With a quiet swish Martin disappeared back underneath the water.

Flint was glad to be feeling better from the effects of the beer and cigarette, but he couldn't totally grasp what had just happened. Perhaps he had just experienced some form of heat stroke, or maybe a hallucination due to the combination of everything. Still the incident felt very real, but he certainly wasn't going to tell anyone about seeing a talking serpent. Instead, he finished out the day and went to bed early that evening.

4

The following day Nadia busied herself unpacking boxes, rearranging furniture, and making a list of items for the pantry. Julie put away her clothes away and positioned her drawing board by the window overlooking the pond. Polly was having the time of her life, chasing packing peanuts and investigating every room and closet. Ethan was busy setting up his office, making calls and catching up on some paperwork.

While everyone was getting settled in, Foster and Faye sneaked out of the house and made their way up the hill to the greenhouse.

Looking in all directions, Foster excitedly professed to Faye, "This place is wonderful with so much mature growth, and these trees are so incredibly tall."

Faye glanced above her head. "I know, we had some very nice trees in England, but this place has so many more."

Foster replied, "No doubt. Look, there's the green house! And wow, an English garden too! It's filled with so many wonderful flowers. And... look... Poppies!"

"Now Foster, those are for admiring – not drinking. Do you understand, mister? You had enough on the trip over here, and we have plenty of work to do."

"Alright, I know, you're right. Look – there's even a vegetable garden and some grape vines too."

Faye and Foster rested in front of the greenhouse and surveyed the grounds. They then closed their eyes and tapped into the vibrations of the surrounding area. With pure thoughts and intentions, they began using their fairy powers to promote the needed support for each plant.

While they busied themselves with this project, they heard soft, guitar playing coming from the parking lot behind the English Garden. Acknowledging the music, they smiled and continued working.

This melodic guitar music was being performed by Flint. He decided to finish out his lunch break in this cool spot while Ryan and Marco went downtown to register for the draft. Since Flint had already registered prior to coming to work, he took this quiet time to practice his guitar.

At the same time, Julie was busy decorating her room with curtains. Since all her bedroom windows were open, she could faintly hear Flint's guitar playing in the distance.

Since music was such a staple part of her previous home, the soothing sounds gave her a comforting feeling. She pondered if she was listening to a recording or someone playing. However, after hearing the music starting and stopping a few times, she concluded it was live. Enjoying the sounds, she continued hanging the curtains. Already Julie was beginning to adapt to her new surroundings.

Foster and Faye were also enjoying the music as they performed their magical ritual. Foster raced over and admired the giant poppy plants with a gigantic grin on his face.

Immediately, Faye gave him a stern look of disapproval that translated to "Get back to work." She worried about him and his close friendship with the milk of the poppy. Foster didn't use it much, but since the journey Faye noticed he was becoming more and more fond of the elixir.

Behind the parking lot was a stone wall that was obscured by some low-hanging tree branches. Unseen by anyone, was a strange young man standing on the wall. He was of average height and looked to be roughly thirty years of age.

From his vantage point, he could see the garden and the main house. He seemed disgusted by the pretty music, so he shifted his glance back to the main house.

He could see Julie standing by her window and found she interested him to no end. He continued watching her with a penetrating, glassy stare.

After several seconds, his blue eyes began to turn completely black with only two small yellow dots in each eye. He then suddenly changed into a large bullfrog and hopped from the wall into the swampy marsh on the other side.

The two fairies finally finished their work in the gardens and stopped to admire their accomplishment. Far away, but getting louder, was the noise of blasting rock music coming up the driveway. Ryan and Marco flew into the greenhouse parking lot and remained seated inside the car.

Quickly Foster whispered to Faye, "It's time for us to exit."

"Yes, I agree." replied Faye.

The two quickly vanished and Flint stopped playing. He put his guitar away and joined the other two.

Mike then arrived in a small golf cart that he used to get from one end of the property to the other. Sitting beside him in the seat was King.

Mike stated, "Well, if it isn't the three stooges. He pointed to King, "Look I've got a friend and he doesn't talk back. Unlike you Marco. You never seem to shut up."

"Screw you, Mike," replied Marco.

Meanwhile, Julie was still finishing hanging her curtains and conversing with Nadia about what color she might like to paint the room. The two went back and forth with ideas, although no decision was made.

Ethan yelled upstairs to Julie and Nadia, "I'm going into town; anybody want to come along?!"

The two girls looked at each other and simultaneously replied, "Yes!"

Due to the heat, all the windows in the main house were wide open. On the outside wall of the living room was the chimney, partially camouflaged by a tall group of rhododendron bushes.

Unseen between the fireplace wall and bushes stood the same strange visitor. He listened to their conversations and smiled when heard Julie's voice. No doubt he was enamored with her looks and wondered how he could intertwine himself into her life.

The two girls ran down the stairs and met Ethan. Julie announced that they were ready to go. Ethan stood there holding a piece of paper in his hand. He then conveyed to Julie and Nadia that he needed to hire a property manager. He explained to them that Mike and the guys did all the grounds work, but he needed someone to live on the property to handle the duties that he himself didn't have time for. Furthermore, this person could live at the gatehouse, oversee operations, and keep an eye on anyone coming into the property.

The strange man overheard this conversation, which gave him an idea on how to become better integrated with this family. He thought to himself; "I'll answer this ad and get this job."

With this thought in mind, he all-of-a-sudden morphed

into a snake and slid down the hill towards the pond. Before submerging into the water, he changed back into a large bullfrog and leaped into the pond.

He was immediately greeted by Martin the serpent. Both floated motionlessly underneath the water in a frozen silence staring at each other. The two then surfaced with only their heads sticking out of the water.

Martin was the first to communicate and resounded, "Who the blazes may I ask are you?"

The frog replied, "I should be asking the same of you. For this is my home, and I wasn't aware that you were invited. My name is Jasper, and I have been dwelling here for the past ten years. You've probably already surmised that I'm not of this earth. The authorities of my dimension have placed me here to serve time and gather information about earth and its inhabitants. My talents allow me to shape shift into any form of animal or human that I wish, although what you see is closest to my true form. My dimension is made up of primarily water, therefore this place suits me fine."

Then Jasper coldly looked at Martin and asked, "Who are you and what is your purpose here?"

Martin elevated a tad higher out of the water, "My name is Martin, and I too have a mission on this planet, but it is not to serve time. Rather it is my job to aid in the development and safety of the family who just purchased this estate. Their well-being is imperative to continue and aid in the advancement of certain people of this earth."

After hearing that, Jasper harshly replied, "Advancement? These inhabitants have no real interest in bettering anything and they never have. Earth people are more concerned about themselves, money, and vanity. This is what I plan to report to my superiors."

Martin recoiled, cocked his head, and winced his eyes at the frog. He replied, "There happens to be many humans that are sensitive and good. Ethan, the new owner, is a decent man that comes from a noble and refined lineage. He and his daughter both have many talents."

The frog glanced towards the main house and with a slanted smile he replied, "Yes, I do like the charming young thing; she is very pretty in a most natural way."

Martin quickly retorted, "That may be so my dear sir, but I warn you; keep your distance or I will be forced to..."

"You'll be forced to do what my friend? Now you listen to me! This is my pond and I'll thank you not to interfere with my work here. Underneath the bridge behind me is a portal that only I can enter or leave. I suggest you stay on your side of the pond and I'll stay on mine." Jasper raised his voice again. "Do I make myself clear Mr. Martin?"

Martin quickly arched back and looked at Jasper in utter disgust. "Well then, good day Jasper! I can't say it's been much of a pleasure, and I repeat – you better keep your distance from this family."

Jasper paid no attention to Martin. Instead, he quickly swam in the direction of the stone bridge, vanishing out of sight.

Martin was somewhat baffled by this strange creature, but he knew well enough to expect more unpleasant situations to arise in the future. He retreated to the other side of the pond and contemplated further about how to deal with this rude character.

5

A few days had passed since Martin and Jasper met and neither had made an appearance to each other or to anyone else. Everyone living and working on the estate had become a little more accustomed to each other.

Earlier in the day, Mike had instructed the guys to start building two rock pillars flanking the end of the cabin road. He was interested to see how things were progressing. Prior to arriving, he slowly approached, and then caught a whiff of smoke that didn't smell like tobacco. Immediately he knew what this smell was and saw that all three boys were passing the peace pipe to each other.

Mike shook his head, and called out, "Working hard I see! Hey Kid, don't puff on any of that stuff. It will rot your brain. However, in Marco's case the damage is already done. Ryan I'm kind of surprised at you, but not really. I thought with you being the oldest you would keep these knuckle heads focused on the job."

"Ah cool your jets, Mike." Ryan replied. "We were just contemplating our next move on the walls."

Mike gave them all a blank stare. "Oh, I get it. If you guys get high enough, you'll be able to levitate the rocks with your minds, right? Alright, the pow wow is over; time to get back to some real work --Ryan get the tractor and attach the trailer to it. Back in the woods there are some old boundary line walls we can steal some rocks from."

Marco yelled back, "Mike, pretty nice job so far, right? Just as good as the ancient slaves that built the pyramids! So, what do you think?"

"Yeah, I have to admit you guys have done a real nice job. Kid, you better put some sunscreen on. It's going to be another scorcher of a day, and you'll end up looking dark as Marco here."

Ryan replied to Mike's comment, "Yeah Marco, you're becoming black as an eggplant."

Marco retorted, "Ah screw you guys, but come to think of it, my package is just as big as..."

Mike interjected with a low tone, "Now listen you guys, there are ladies about so watch your tongues. Furthermore, let me tell you something. I work part-time at the Veteran's hospital; and black or white, they all come in different shapes and sizes."

Meanwhile King sat in the golf cart listening to this conversation, reading each one of the boys. After gathering his impressions, he decided he liked Flint the best. Flint reminded him of Ethan. He had the same quiet, observant nature and no doubt looked British.

Flint loved all animals, so he approached King and gave him a couple pets and a squeezed his big neck. His thoughtful act confirmed to King that he was a right about Flint and believed him to be a trusted soul.

Now that everyone had left the area, Flint looked over in the direction of the pond in the distance. He still couldn't believe the bizarre encounter he had with Martin the serpent. Though he had a highly active imagination, a talking sea monster that seemed to know everything about him was way beyond his normal fantasies. He asked himself if this creature was just a manifestation of his cigarette induced nausea, or if there was something living in that pond? Still curious, he started walking towards the pond.

Then from around the corner of the bath house came the snapping, chugging sound of the tractor. Ryan yelled at Flint to jump into the trailer. Then they both disappeared into the tall trees to find more rocks for the walls.

Back at the main house Ethan was sitting on the back patio reading the paper when the phone rang from inside the house. Putting the paper down, he briskly moved into the house, pondering who could be calling. He then remembered that it might be a reply about the caretaker position. At the same time Julie and Nadia appeared from different ends of the house. The phone hadn't rung since they had arrived, and everyone was curious who it could be. After the fifth ring Ethan lifted the receiver and replied, "Clark residence."

A man answered with a southern accent, "Good afternoon. My name is Jasper Benton, and I'm callin' regarding your ad for the caretaker position." Without pause he continued, "I've just arrived in the area. See, I'm originally from Oklahoma and I believe this position is right up my alley. Before arriving in New York, I worked on a large ranch back home. Frankly, there's nothing I don't know how to do when it comes to taking care of grounds, buildings, and animals. I do have some references and would like to meet with y'all as soon as possible."

Ethan's first reaction was this guy was a bit long winded, but he sounded eager and perfect for the position. He replied, "Jasper... my name is Ethan Clark. My daughter and housekeeper both live with me here on the estate. We have recently relocated here from England so my daughter can attend school in New York City. There is a full-time gardener and a handful of workers that come during the day to maintain the grounds. I would like very much

to meet with you and discuss exactly what I'm looking for. How about tomorrow evening, say around seven
o'clock?"

Jasper eagerly replied, "Well, I would be delighted to do
so. It's a date; I'll be there seven o'clock sharp."

As Ethan placed the receiver down, both Julie and Nadia
stood beside him bug-eyed and curious. Julie asked her
father, "I thought Mike was the caretaker as well as the
gardener?"

"Yes, Julie, Mike does quite a bit around here, but as
I explained before I need someone who can manage the
place when I'm not here. Now that we are settled, I plan
to make a few trips back to England. As a matter of fact, I
heard from your grandmother, and it seems she and your
grandfather are missing us terribly. Since there's plenty
of room here, I've offered them to live here."

Julie's eyes lit up with excitement and exclaimed, "That
would be super! Grandpa Eric can be a bit stiff at times,
but Grandma Victoria is such a trip. After all, she knows
so much about plants and flowers. The two of them
would absolutely love it here. We could redecorate the
cabin and have them live there!"

Nadia joyfully chimed in and said, "Yes, the more the
merrier."

Ethan grinned, "Then it's settled. I'll plan to fly back this
week and escort them back. Also, Ian wants me to help
him remodel his kitchen and I told him I would."

Smiles grew on everyone's faces, and they all divided
and resumed their duties.

6

Everything was coming together for the family in the main house. At the same time, members of a much smaller household were being prepared. Faye and Foster had discovered a crawl space in the peak of the greenhouse roof.

The greenhouse was split into two sections. One section was the glassed portion for the plants, and the other was a combination of brick, cement, and wood construction.

In the second section were several windows, a sink, and some storage cabinets. Inside at the top of largest cabinet was a trap door that opened to the peak of the roof; it was up there that they decided to make their humble abode. Since this space had never been used and was virtually out of site, it provided safety from Polly or any other intruder.

After arranging their living quarters, with wide eyes and a big grin, Foster turned to Faye. "So, my dear, you have done such a wonderful job with this space. I think we should take a break and see how everyone else is getting along."

Faye smiled back, "Just give me a few more moments to make up the bed, and then we shall explore."

"Sounds good," Foster replied. "But I think we should avoid the bridge at the north end of the pond."

With a curious look on her face, Faye replied, "Why do you say that?"

"Well, do you remember the feeling I had when we first arrived here? I still get that funny feeling at times, but I can't seem to put my finger on just what it is."

Faye retorted, "I think you're still having flashbacks from all of the poppy milk you ingested on the way here."

"Perhaps," replied Foster. "But I know there is something strange and inhuman residing over there."

"If you think so, dear. Alright, I'm ready. Let's go."

"Yes, but we must be careful not to let any of the workers see us and must certainly watch out for Miss Polly. I don't think she would eat us, but she would get a thrill chasing us up a tree."

Joyfully the two wandered down the driveway to the main house. They could hear laughing and the clanging of tools off in the distance.

Foster and Faye walked past the main house and down the slate pathway to the bath house. They spotted the three guys on the other side of the property putting the finishing touches on the stone pillars they had been erecting.

Faye commented, "Now there's a lively bunch, especially the Italian-looking fellow. Look! There's the young man who was playing his guitar. You know it looks to me that the older boys seem to be more cutout for this type of work, whereas the younger one seems to be a little out of place."

"I agree," said Foster. "But there's nothing wrong with a

little hard work. After all, he is noticeably young. I think if he continues playing his guitar, he may touch many with his talent someday."

"You're so observant, my dear. This chatter and noise are annoying me. Let's take a stroll by the pond – shall we?"

"Capitol idea, my dear. I now feel inclined to investigate that area at over by the bridge."

"With a frown Faye replied, "There you go again with your feelings, Mr. spooky pants."

As they approached the pond, the blue sky reflected in the calm water. Dragonflies buzzed erratically back and forth between the flowering waterlilies.

The fairies now stood at the edge of the pond with their eyes closed, taking in all the beauty. Then, all-of-a-sudden, a large splash of water soaked them, snapping them out of their meditation.

Martin made his grand appearance, now peering down at them. Frozen with surprise and shock, they stood before him with their jaws dropped in awe.

Martin grinned and announced, "Greetings you two. My name is Martin, and I have been with Ethan and his family since he was a boy. My apologies for this abrupt intrusion, but It is urgent that I reveal myself to the both of you. I'm afraid that all of us are facing a rather menacing force on this property."

Both fairies stood dumbfounded by Martin's presence. Faye, was the first to speak, "Please to meet you, Mr. Martin."

Foster quickly turned facing Faye with bulging eyes. "See, dear, I told you something wasn't right here. He looks familiar too."

Faye stared at Foster. "Yes, so you said." She looked back at Martin and asked, "Just what or who are you referring to?"

In a hushed voice Martin explained, "On the other side

of this pond is queer sort of creature that has the power to morph into whatever he pleases. This rude creature is extremely negative and threatened me. I feel we all need to be wary of this character. He calls himself Jasper and claims to be placed here from another dimension to gather information and God knows what else."

Foster's head was spinning. "Now, just hold on. You say you've been watching over Ethan all these years? Why haven't you made yourself known before? We've been with him and his family for some time now!"

"My dear man, I apologize for dishing you all this information at once. Please allow me to explain. Ethan's lineage goes back to centuries ago in Scotland. His great grandfather was from an extremely high order of knights that protected and provided for the early tribes of the land. My kind was placed on Earth from another star system to aid and assist the development of these knights. My elders were aware that these men had many talents and a willingness to do good for the earth.

Martin paused for a moment. "You see, my kind can communicate on deep levels with humans. We observe their problems and hard-ships and assist when needed. You wouldn't have seen me because I exist primarily in the water. I have always been with this family and will do whatever I must to protect them.

Faye shook her head to Martin. "We too have a fondness and connection to Ethan and Julie. As you know Ethan lost his beloved Sarah, and we refuse to move on until he has adjusted to her loss."

Foster interjected, "He still is in pain, but we both felt moving to this place would be a positive new start. However, this Jasper could really throw a wrench into things."

Martin replied, "You are quite right, but it's not Ethan I'm worried about; it's his daughter Julie. This creature has his eye on Julie. Therefore, we must do all we can to protect her. Don't you both agree?"

Foster and Faye faced each other and simultaneously nodded their heads in agreement.

Martin leaned down and whispered to Faye and Foster. "I have introduced myself to Flint, but I'm not sure he's convinced of our meeting. After all, I do have that effect on humans."

Faye replied, "You took us by surprise as well, but we are glad to have finally met you. We are also grateful for your service to this family."

Foster quickly blared out, "I had a dream with you in it!"

Faye gave him a quick jab to his side, and continued, "Where is Jasper now and how will we know if it's him when we encounter him?"

Martin explained, "His natural form is that of a large, man-sized bullfrog, but it seems he has to retreat to his portal on the other side of the pond under the bridge. I'm afraid I can't say what form he will take next; I suppose he could pose himself as any one of us."

Foster gave Faye a hard glance, and whispered, "See, I told you."

Martin stared back at the two fairies. "Then it's settled. We shall meet here as often as possible to discuss our plans and observations. I believe we also have another adversary on our side, the young worker Flint. He too shares a similar heritage to that of Ethan, and I know he finds young Julie attractive."

Foster agreed, "We've both observed this young man too, and we sense good things about him. He and the Gardener Mike seem to be close. We will plan to contact Mike and see if he can find some way help to bring Flint and Julie together."

Martin finished, "The more I learn about this fellow, the better. We'll keep each other informed going forward." He gave them a warm smile and instantly disappeared into the pond.

Immediately after Martin left the dragonflies resumed their activity, and everything returned to normal.

Foster turned to Faye with an exaggerated look on his face. "Never a dull moment Aye?"

"Oh brother," Faye replied. "Here I thought we would only be taking care of flowers, and now this! I told you we have a purpose here, and our best work is yet to come."

7

By now the interior construction for bath house was nearly completed. The only thing remaining to be done was the painting of the walls. This job was skillfully handled by Karl and Karl, a pair of Polish gentlemen in their late thirties who looked remarkably similar but weren't related. The main difference was one Karl was considerably taller than the other. Marco, Ryan, and Flint had become well acquainted with them but found the language barrier a bit challenging at times. Nevertheless, Marco could easily communicate with the use of sign language and body motions emulating the act of having sex in one form or another.

Karl and Karl were both finishing up for the day when Nadia walked in with a stack of freshly folded bath towels. Instantly, the taller Karl struck up a conversation with her asking where she grew up and how long she had been with the family.

Their conversation was interrupted when a pair of gentlemen knocked on one of the French doors of the bath house. They had several large boxes that contained stereo equipment, wires, and speakers. Nadia excused herself and then let them in.

The first delivery man introduced himself. "Good afternoon, we're here to install the stereo system."

Nadia opened the door wider and gestured for them to come in. "Of course. Do what you must; just don't leave a big mess for me, alright?"

"Sure, miss, this won't take too long." answered the installer.

Ethan loved listening to music, so he ordered a nice high-end reel-to-reel, receiver, amplifier, and multiple speakers to be installed in the bath house.

Nadia left with a big smile on her face and found it refreshing to speak her native tongue again after such a long time. No doubt, she and tall Karl had hit it off.

Both the painters and the stereo installers finished and left for the day. The painting was almost done, and the new stereo system was now installed.

Later that afternoon, Flint and Mike were busy sweeping the back patio of the main house. Flint had heard the testing of the sound system earlier and was curious to check it out before leaving for the day. He decided to take a brake and walk down to the bath house. Flint poked his head in the door and walked over to the large closet that housed the sound system.

After assessing the gear, he saw that the reel-to-reel had a set of microphone inputs. He was thrilled at the notion that maybe Mr. Clark would let him record his guitar playing. Before leaving for the day Flint approached Mike and asked, "Do you think you could talk to Mr. Clark about letting me record my guitar on the stereo system?"

Mike gave him one of his non-emotional blank stares, paused for a moment and said, "Sure kid, I'll ask him. He seems like a nice enough guy. I'll see what I can do for ya'. I don't really understand your kind of music, but it sounds peaceful – not like the shit Marco and Ryan listen to. I'll talk to him tomorrow and see what he says."

Mike smiled at Flint and placed his hand on his shoulder, "You did a real nice job today kid. I think you have what they call a green thumb. Seems to me you're more cut out for this kind of work than the heavier stuff."

Flint agreed and replied, "I'd rather be playing my guitar instead of slaving in the hot sun eight hours a day."

Mike cocked his head and looked him in the eye. "I know kid, but hard work is good for the soul and the music business can be a harder road than this one. I've worked all kinds of jobs and dealt with a variety of assholes and sons-of-bitches, and you know something? It's nice to be left alone with my thoughts and nature. When you're older, you'll look back and realize what I'm talking about."

Flint momentarily meditated on what Mike had just told him, and a few seconds later replied, "Yeah, I guess so Mike, but my knees feel differently right at the moment."

Mike replied, "Alright, tomorrow's another day. Don't get too polluted with those other two knuckle heads tonight. It's going to be another hot day tomorrow, and a hangover doesn't make it go by any faster. Do you know what I'm saying?"

"Yeah, your right." replied Flint. "See you in the morning, Mike."

8

By this time, Julie was attending classes and getting acclimated to her busy schedule. Overall, she was thrilled with America and to be enrolled in such a wonderful school. However, she found the hustle of the city was quite the contrast to rural England.

That afternoon Julie caught the express from Grand Central Station to Croton-Harmon where she would be met and picked up by Nadia. The express was perfect because it had less stops. It gave her a chance to decompress and maybe even catch a few quick winks.

As the train breezed pass most of the local stops, Julie thought about her studies. She gazed out the train window and admired the clear blue sky that reflected in the water. The brilliance of the setting sun gave the Hudson River a sparkling champagne appearance.

After a couple of short stops, she found herself dosing to the faint, syncopated drum-like clacking of the train wheels rolling on the tracks. She remained asleep during the longest stint between stops until she was abruptly awakened by the whooshing noise of the train car opening.

The windblown conductor entered the car, appearing somewhat drunk due to the motion of the train, although the off chance he could have had a few nips wouldn't be stretching the truth. The conductor refitted his cap on his head and announced loudly. "Croton-Harmon next and last stop! For those passengers continuing to Poughkeepsie, you will need to exit and switch trains!"

Startled, and somewhat bleary-eyed, Julie switched her attention back to the river. She then spotted what appeared to be a green hump protruding from the water near the shore. Not giving it much thought, she looked over to the opposite seat to see if anyone else had seen what she did.

To her surprise there sat a rather peculiar young man. However, this man's gaze was not out the window, but directly at Julie. She momentarily looked directly into his eyes, and for a split second they looked very dark with tiny yellow dots. She blinked and then the man's eyes instantly changed to blue. Feeling a bit ill at ease, she quickly returned her gaze back out the train window. She decided to continue watching the water to discourage any further interaction or communication with this odd passenger. She attributed his weird eyes to just waking from a nap combined with the light reflecting on his face.

The strange man seemed to be in his mid-thirties. He had blonde wavy hair, a long face with a chiseled chin. He wore casual attire consisting of hush puppy shoes, khaki pants, and a checkered button-down collar shirt. At first,

Julie found this young man somewhat handsome, but at the same time he exuded a strange vibe unlike anything she had ever experienced before.

Just at that second the train door opened from the rear of the car. The conductor walked down the aisle swaying from side to side retrieving the ticket stubs from the seats. He loudly announced, "Croton-Harman last and final stop, this way out."

Julie rapidly gathered her portfolio and handbag. Then she quickly followed directly behind the conductor, making sure not to look in any direction but forward. Once she arrived at the door of the train, she glanced back surveying the entire coach, but there was no sign of this person. Relieved, she exited the train and was welcomed by Nadia's huge grin and big brown eyes.

Nadia's intoxicating perfume which usually overwhelmed Julie was much welcome on this occasion. The two quickly walked up the stairs chatting between them as they headed for the parking lot.

Ethan was seated in his classroom reading some journals when there was a knock on the door. Standing at the opening was a tall young student with several books tucked under his arm.

"Excuse me, Mr. Clark," uttered the young man. "I was wondering if you could spare a few minutes of your time. My name is Cleveland Douglas. I'm from your fifth period class."

Ethan halted from what he was reading and looked up. "Hello. Yes, I'm glad to see you. I really need to pull myself away from these journals. What can I do for you?"

Cleveland answered, "Well, I'm extremely interested in what you thought of my paper? I know you're busy and stuff, but it's especially important that I pass this course because if I don't then..."

Ethan raised both his hands in front of his face and interrupted him mid-sentence. "Cleveland, I was going to speak with you tomorrow. However, now that your here, I have some good news, and some bad news; first the bad news. Your sentence structure needs some work, which I can help you with. Now for the good news. Your essay's content is the best I've read in my seventeen years of teaching. What you have executed here is a very inspiring and sensitive piece of writing."

Cleveland's face changed from a sheepish expression to that of a boy who just received a new car. "Oh, wow, Mr. Clark you really thought it was that good?"

"As a matter of fact, it borders on great," Ethan replied. He continued. "I want you to succeed, but you'll have to spend some extra hours with me to brush up on a few things. If you're willing to put in the time, I guarantee you will definitely pass this course."

Cleveland advanced towards Ethan grabbing his hand and giving it a vigorous shake. He joyfully replied, "Yes sir, thank you."

Ethan slipped the pile of journals into his briefcase, "Alright then, meet me after class tomorrow and I'll show you a few tricks to help you excel in your work."

Quickly looking at his watch Ethan's eyes bulged and announced, "Oh boy look at the time. I have got to get going; remember tomorrow and don't let me down Mr. Douglas."

"I won't. You must be the coolest teacher I've ever had. You know – everyone else says the same too. It's like I'm learning from my favorite uncle or something; don't ever change Mr. Clark."

Buy this time Ethan had his coat on and was on his way out the door. He passed the young man wearing a wide grin and ran down the hallway. Ethan planned to meet with the potential caretaker Jasper, so he hurried home to beat the rush hour traffic.

Later that evening Nadia was clearing the table after serving her delicious Hungarian goulash. Ethan and Julie both raved to her how wonderful it was. She winked her eye and said, "It is a secret recipe handed down from my great grandmother. I can't tell you the ingredients, but it has to do with just the right spice blend."

Nadia smiled at Julie and Ethan, "So, how are the two of you doing with school? I mean Julie, your studies, and Mr. Clark, how is teaching going?"

They both looked up and answered at the same time, "Great."

Nadia nodded and gazed back at them. "That's nice. You know, I've been having some wonderful conversations with Karl, the painter."

"Which one?" Ethan replied.

"Oh, the tall Karl. He is nice, and we know many of the same places in Poland."

Julie looked up and said, "Nadia, do I see a twinkle in your eye?"

Nadia tilted her head to one side. "Yes, he is very buff and handsome. We are planning to go out to dinner tomorrow night and maybe go out dancing too."

Nadia now somewhat blushed, quickly changed the conversation. "How about you, Julie. Have you met anyone at school yet?"

Julie scraped the last few bites out of her bowl and looked up. "Well, no I haven't. With so much homework I'm finding it a challenge to find time for anything else."

Ethan was aware that Julie's mood had changed so he chimed in, "By all means, Julie, schoolwork comes first. Perhaps once you've acclimated you can shake your tail feathers a little."

THE SERPENT OF WOODLANDS

Julie turned her head and rolled her eyes upward. "Yes father." She quickly changed the subject, "By the way dad, are the boys going to be working here on the weekend too?"

Ethan picked up the cloth napkin and wiped some gravy from the corner of his mouth. "No, they are only here Monday through Friday. Mike stops in briefly on Saturday mornings, but if this new caretaker Jasper works out, he won't have to do that anymore. As a matter of fact, this guy should be here in a few minutes."

Just at that moment there were three slow knocks on the front door. Ethan rose from the table, throwing his napkin down and shouted to Nadia who was in the kitchen. "Could you get the front door please. Tell the man I'll be there momentarily!"

Ethan then whispered to Julie, "I have to throw down a *Tums* really quick; must be those secret spices."

Julie remained seated at the table, but from her vantage point she still had a clear view of the front door. Nadia pulled open the door and gracefully greeted the man. "Please come in."

Jasper politely wiped his shoes and stood before Nadia. She towered over him more than a foot which placed her large bust in direct line with his face. Jasper found her delightful, but her perfume made his eyes tear slightly.

Julie decided to quickly peek at the man, and, to her surprise, she recognized him immediately. She remembered the man's shirt, his pants and hair. "That's the guy who was on the train, she said to herself." At that instant, and somewhat stunned, she decided not to meet this person. Julie quickly and quietly scooped up Polly and made a fast jaunt up the stairs to her bedroom.

At that same moment Ethan popped out of the bathroom and walked to the front door. He approached Jasper and extended his hand. "So, you're Jasper. I'm Ethan Clark. Thanks for coming. Please come into the living room and have a seat. Can I get you something to drink?"

Speaking in a slow Oklahoman drawl, he replied, "Why, that would genuinely nice. I'm kind of dry from all this heat we've had lately. Not that it's not dry where I come from, but a cold beverage would be most welcome."

Some light conversation was exchanged between Ethan and Jasper. After a short spell, the two of them and King left in the golf cart to take a quick tour of the buildings and grounds.

Jasper pretended to look interested and was able to make Ethan believe that it was his first time visiting the estate. Unknown to Ethan, Jasper was a cold and calculating creature whose sole plan was to win Julie's affection.

Ethan had much on his mind, thinking about his upcoming plans to fly back to England. He didn't have the time to wait for more responses from his ad, so he hired Jasper and invited him to stay at the gatehouse for evening.

Overall, Ethan found Jasper to have all the necessary qualifications and felt he would at least give him a try. They both shook hands again and then separated.

Ethan wanted to let Julie and Nadia know of his decision. When Ethan and King returned to the main house, Julie and Nadia were sitting in the living room chatting away. King ran between Ethan's legs, nearly causing him to trip and fall. King's intent was to find Polly for some reason.

Ethan sat down with them and explained that he decided to give Jasper a try. "I wanted you both to have a say. So, what do you think?"

Nadia replied, "Fine with me. He seems alright. He's a good-looking man, but he is quite different. Maybe it's his accent. I've never met a southern American before."

Ethan replied, "Yes, he has a peculiar demeanor, but we'll see how he does for month or so. Julie, what do you think? I sense you have some mixed feelings about this man."

Expressionless Julie just peered at the floor and said, "Well. I'm not totally sure. He seems alright, but I can't really explain my reservations. Sorry Dad."

Julie didn't want to discuss anything about what she had experienced on the train. After all, she only saw him for several seconds and then he was gone. The thought crossed her mind that perhaps she had mistaken Jasper for the stranger, but the shirt and the pants were all the same.

Again, Julie rationalized that she had just awakened from her nap. The thing with his eyes and the creepy feeling was just a result of an exhausting day.

Without going into any further discussion, Julie looked up and smiled, "Dad whatever you wish to do is fine. I have plenty of schoolwork to do, and we also need to start getting things ready for Grandpa Eric and Grandma Victoria." Julie excused herself and went into the bathroom.

King had gone from room to room, trying to locate Polly and was intent on communicating to her about this Jasper guy. King was a particularly good judge of character, but his dog sense was confused to say the least. He thought, there's something fake about this man, and now I've got to get a take from a cat's point of view. With four good leaps he bounded up the stairs and made his way into Julie's room.

Polly was curled in a ball at the base of Julie's bed. She raised her head, giving King a piercing look. "Now what on earth do you want? Seems you're always hanging with that man Mike and the other three. Now what's with the grand entrance and before you start, catch your breath and sit the hell down."

King collected himself. "Look, Missy, we've got to be on guard with this new caretaker. I can't put my paw on it, but there is something very odd about this fellow. All I'm saying is keep your eyes open and let me know what you think when you see him."

Polly stopped licking her paw and stared back at King. "Oh, alright big guy, I trust your instincts. Now go clean yourself up, you stink."

9

Several days passed and Mike arrived earlier than usual to scope out a nice overgrown patch of pachysandra. The bank that separated the main house from the lower lawn had some old juniper bushes that needed replacing. He figured everybody could stay cool in the forest while gathering the ground cover.

Mike walked over to the shed structure that housed the golf cart and stumbled upon King. King knew what was coming next, so he jumped into the passenger seat. Mike turned to King and gave him a pat on the head and took off towards the main house.

Currently, Ethan was just exiting the house, carrying his suitcase and shoulder bag. He was about to leave for the airport. Ethan was a bit taken back by the abrupt appearance of the battery-driven golf cart and with a wide-eyed expression exclaimed, "Oh, good morning Mike."

Rolling to a stop and wearing a friendly smile, Mike replied, "Certainly is a good morning. Are you heading out for your journey across the drink?"

Ethan put his suitcase and bag down, "Mike you're just the guy I wanted to see. I have several things to go over with you before leaving. First, I wanted to let you know that you and the boys are doing a fine job, and everything looks great."

Mike nodded and replied, "Well after fifteen years, you get the routine down and know what needs to be done."

"Yes of course. As you know I'm flying back to England to escort my parents to the states. Going forward they'll be setting up permanent residence here on the estate. In my absence there will be a need for someone to look after my personal affairs and keep an eye on the place during the evening hours. Therefore, I've hired a man to take care of such things. His name is Jasper; he's a transient from Oklahoma who claims to be a jack-of-all-trades. The man is somewhat strange but seems likable and competent. I'm giving him a try while I'm gone, so I'm counting on you to give me a report when I return. He'll be staying in the gatehouse, and I believe he plans to connect with you later today. Otherwise just keep doing what you guys do and I'll see you on my return. Oh, and please check in on Nadia and Julie every so often. I would greatly appreciate that."

"It would be my pleasure, sir." Mike joyfully replied. "And, by the way, the kid, I mean Flint, asked me if he could use your stereo system to record some of his guitar playing. He seems to know how to use these things, but I told him I'd ask your permission first."

"Yes, Julie mentioned him to me. I understand he plays a real sweet guitar; she's enjoyed listening to him play. I don't see why not. After all I'm a musician myself and certainly like to encourage the Fine Arts. Tell him it would be alright, as long as he is careful with the equipment and allows me to listen to the recording when he's done."

Mike nodded his head slowly. "Will do, Mr. Clark. Thank you and have a safe and enjoyable trip."

10

L ater that morning Mike had returned from the woods after finding a nice harvesting spot of pachysandra. Grabbing a shovel, Mike walked over to the bank to inspect the juniper bushes that needed to be removed. After surmising the project, he decided to have a seat and enjoy a morning smoke before the boys arrived.

The water in the pond was still with just a small amount of morning fog floating above the water. Mike gave some thought about the new guy, this Oklahoman named Jasper. His concentration was broken by the sound of two splashes coming from either end of the pond. Mike's head darted from one side to other as if he were watching a tennis match. He saw nothing and figured it to be a couple catfish feeding from the banks of the pond. However, unbeknownst to him, the two splashing noises were made by both Martin and Jasper.

Martin was moving slightly above the water, as he watched Mike from an unseen vantage point. At the same time, Jasper had parked the truck by the stone bridge, morphed to his frog-like identity, and jumped in the water.

A few seconds later Mike heard the faint sound of music getting louder as it approached the main house. This time he knew exactly who and where this was coming from.

Ryan's car came flying up the driveway. The music quickly shut off as the car pulled into the parking area by the greenhouse. Marco and Ryan crawled out of the car, arguing about who was the best guitar player.

Mike quickly dismissed the noises coming from the pond. He stood up and turned. To his astonishment, he saw Foster and Faye standing next to one of the juniper shrubs. He stepped back, in disbelief of the two creatures standing before him.

Since the fairies had never revealed themselves to any human, they too were frozen with fear. Mike dropped to his knees from the fascination of seeing the fairies. He cocked his head and whispered, "Are you two what I think you are?"

Foster was about to speak when Faye halted him. "My dear sweet man, you are not hallucinating. We are both very real." With this announcement Faye had Mike's full attention. "We came here with Mr. Clark from England, and yes, we are fairies. I understand this is a surprise, but we needed to make our presence known. Even Ethan doesn't know of our existence, but there can be no further delay in explaining what you should know." Faye paused to catch her breath and compose herself.

Foster stepped forward. "You see, there is a malevolent force at work on these grounds, and the man that has come to stay here is not what he appears to be."

Mike rubbed both of his eyes, cleared his throat, and shook his head slowly back and forth. "Now I've been on this planet for fifty-two years, fought in the war, and was even fairly sure I saw one of those flying saucers once. But this beats all."

Faye interjected once again, "Mr. Mike, there really isn't enough time to explain everything to you right now. However, you should know that we have been with Ethan and Julie for quite some time. And just yesterday we were introduced to another non-human part of Ethan's family. Forgive me for rambling, but I fear the other workers are approaching. We shall continue this conversation at another time. It's important that you keep a close eye on Julie. Be extremely cautious of this man named Jasper. I'm afraid he has an unpleasant agenda that somehow includes her."

Mike thought the combination of his age and the heat must have finally caught up with him. Nonetheless, there on the ground right before him stood two very real fairies. Quickly collecting himself Mike replied, "Alright, you two, I'm reading you loud and clear. I'll do my best to understand what has just taken place here, but you've got some more explaining to do."

Foster cocked his head at Mike. "You have a good soul, I can tell. You and Flint are incredibly special human beings. We have observed this and ask that you help young Flint to become better acquainted with Julie. Both of you are her only protection from this man... this thing."

Faye raised her head and put her finger to her lips to quiet the conversation. "The boys are approaching; we must go now."

Mike could hear the voices of three boys rounding the corner of the main house. Ryan and Marco were still in a heated debate about who was the best rock n' roll guitarist. Mike looked back to the ground, but the fairies had vanished.

The boys stopped talking and stared at Mike. He quickly stood to his feet and immediately took hold of the conversation. "Gentlemen, we have another scorcher of a day ahead, so I've come up with a plan for us to beat the heat. We'll still have the bugs, but the project I have in mind will keep us out of the sun for a spell."

With a mouth full of hard roll Marco looked at Mike

and said, "I've got a good idea. Let's raid the wine cellar, chill out in the pool, and crank up some tunes on that new sound system." Marco then followed that statement by bobbing his head while poised in a classic air-guitar stance. With coffee splashing from his cup, he then lifted his leg and let out a huge loud fart.

Mike looked back at him with a half-smile combined with an air of disgust, and replied, "No, I don't think so. I shouldn't have to remind you that there are women nearby."

Now that he had everybody's attention, Mike lowered his voice and motioned his arms for everybody to huddle. "Now listen, Mr. Clark has already left for the airport to catch his flight to England. I believe he'll be gone for about two weeks. Seems he's gone ahead and hired a caretaker to stay at the gatehouse. This person has been hired to oversee the operations and handle some of Mr. Clark's personal affairs while he's gone."

Marco winced his eyes and blared out, "We don't take orders from some newcomer. Besides, we've all been here for a while, and know what we got to do. This is fucking bullshit!"

Mike interjected, "Now calm down. Let's meet this guy and find out what he's like. Apparently, he's from Oklahoma, and claims to be a jack of all trades. His name is Jasper."

Marco leaned forward, spit on the ground and said, "His name is shit."

"Calm down, Curly." remarked Ryan. "There are four of us and one of him. Mike's right. Let's find out how this Oakie measures up."

Flint remained quiet, shifting his glance to each person that spoke.

Mike nodded in agreement. "You're exactly right, Ryan. Now let's get to work. Mr. Clark said Jasper would come and meet us at some point today." The crew dispersed and Marco and Ryan left together to fetch the tracker.

Mike stopped Flint and pulled him aside. "Now Kid, I spoke with Mr. Clark about letting you use the stereo system. He didn't have a problem with it but asked that you be careful. He also wants to hear what you've done when you're finished. I think that's mighty nice of him so be incredibly careful with that equipment. If you bust that piece of gear, you'll be working for free until next winter."

Smiling from ear to ear, Flint thanked Mike and assured him that he would be cautious.

Mike lit a cigarette and looked Flint in the eyes. "I think we are all in for an interesting day. Now I've got to go and get some shovels. I want you to start pulling the weeds and dead leaves from underneath those juniper shrubs so we can easily wrap the chains around the base of them."

Flint put his gloves on, knelt and began to perform the task. He was alone when he heard a splashing noise coming from the direction of the pond. He stood back up and surveyed the length of the pond. Once again, a loud splash resounded from the far-left corner of the pond.

Flint then ran down the bank to see what all the noise was. To his astonishment there was Martin elevated several feet out of the water, smiling and staring at him.

A strange feeling came over Flint as he uncontrollably moved closer to the serpent. His first encounter was very ethereal, but this time he was unaffected and very much sober. Flint was now convinced that Martin was real, and this serpent was no hallucination.

Martin was the first to speak in a loud whisper. "Come closer at once, young man."

Flint looked side to side to see if anyone else was around. He slowly approached Martin and was once again entranced by Martin's human-like mannerisms and expressions.

Flint opened his mouth to speak when Martin interjected, "My dear boy. I have a very urgent favor to ask of

you. Please listen carefully. This new man who calls himself Jasper is someone to be leery of."

Martin sank lower in the water and moved closer to
Flint. "He is not of this world. Well, neither am I, but this
creature is from a quite different dimension. You must
understand he's not to be trusted. Whatever you do, don't
let him or anyone else know you're onto this fact. This
creature is a shape shift-er and I'm afraid he's only after
one thing; Ethan's daughter, Julie."

Flint's head was overloaded by Martin's urgency, but he
felt willing to do whatever he could. He, too, had a strong
attraction for Julie and didn't wish anything bad to happen to her.

Martin extended himself back out of the water, posi-
tioning his face just above Flint's. Some small droplets of
water dripped on Flint's head.

Martin spoke in a calming tone. "Flint, my son, you
must have the courage to overcome your shyness and get
to know Julie better. She likes you. I can tell – especially
your guitar playing. Do your best to keep her safe while
Ethan is away in England. I must follow him for as I mentioned before, he is my responsibility. I am assigning you
the job of guarding his daughter. Are you up for the task,
young man?"

Flint looked up at Martin, thinking he wouldn't dare say
no to the responsibility. He replied, "I'll do my best. But
tell me, how can I compete with a shape-shifting being
from another dimension?"

Martin looked into Flint's eyes. "My boy, you have hon-
esty, creativity and plenty of power. You just don't know
it yet. This Jasper must slowly gain Julie's confidence.
He's not going to jeopardize his status so soon. You'll be
alright. Just keep your ears and eyes open, and I'll be back
soon. Now, remember what I told you. Get to know Julie.
Ask her out. She is new here and doesn't know anybody.
I'm counting on you. Do your best, and I'll see you soon,

my lad." With a flash of green light, Martin disappeared into the water.

Just then Mike returned and saw Flint peering into the pond in a frozen stare. He yelled down to Flint. "Hey Kid, you're on the clock! Let's get cracking. It's not getting any cooler out!"

Flint rallied himself and returned to clearing the brush around the junipers. While doing so he reflected on the responsibility that had just been bestowed on him. He thought to himself. "How am I ever going to make any kind of impression on a wealthy and pretty young girl? And this serpent creature, whatever it is. Why does he think I can save this girl?"

Nonetheless, now wasn't time to figure out how to deal with all these perplexing demands. Instead, he pulled himself together and continued the task at hand.

Currently, Jasper was at the gatehouse preparing himself for his first meeting with the work crew. He already knew who each of them was but needed to somehow convince them that he was a real handyman. Jasper thought that to be one of the guys, he would have to come up with a few stories or jokes that they could identify with. Jasper knew above all he needed to show them who was in charge. After all, Mr. Clark was depending on him to see that everything ran smoothly in his absence. Then the image of young Julie came to the forefront of his mind. Jasper figured, with that old 'fish n' chips' serpent out of the way, she should be pretty easy prey.

Jasper's time in this dimension was soon to end. He would have gathered all the information that was required of him and paid his debt. In turn, he would reward himself with young Julie and do whatever he wished with her. With this thought a tight-lipped smile in the form of a crescent moon grew upon his face.

The temperature had climbed to ninety-five degrees, and the guys were on their knees planting behind the main house. Everyone's arms and faces were smudged with dirt from wiping away the mosquitoes and black flies.

Jasper moved slowly up the incline of the driveway before parking in front of the main house. He turned off the engine and straightened his cowboy hat and put on his mirror aviator sunglasses. He got out of the truck and quickly walked around to the back of the house to meet the guys.

Once he arrived, everyone stopped working and slowly stood up from their crouched positions. They all stared back at Jasper with blank, non-emotional looks on their faces.

Jasper smiled to break the tension and confidently approached each of one of them by shaking their hands and introducing himself. Jasper pushed his hat higher away from his forehead and said, "Sure is a scorcher out here today; y'all look like some kind of prison chain gang."

Marco was the first to speak and piped up, "Yeah, except we're free to go anytime we wish, isn't that right Mike?"

Mike gave Marco a piercing sideways glance, imploring him to cool his jets. He then replied to Jasper, "The heat gets to one's head, and I think this is a good time for us to take a break and get better acquainted. What do you say, gentleman?"

The shovels dropped to the ground, and everybody brushed the dirt from their clothes and took a seat on the patio chairs. Mike pulled out one his *Pall Mall* cigarettes and silently offered one to Jasper. Jasper shook his head and Marco tapped Mike on the shoulder and said, "I'll take one of those bug repellents if you don't mind."

If it had been lunch time, Ryan would have busted into one of his colorful stories, but instead he sat quietly reading Jasper through his sun squinted eyes.

Flint stared ahead, maintaining his quiet composure but all the while keeping his cerebral radar on high alert.

Marco asked Jasper what Oklahoma was like and how the women looked down there. He continued, "So, Jasper, you got yourself a local squeeze, or you just do the bar scene?"

Jasper went along with him a came up with a story he knew everybody would get a kick out of. He dropped his mirror sunglasses and made eye contact with the crew and proceeded to tell his tale. "No, I don't have a regular girl right now, but I did have a rather interesting and rather embarrassing run-in last week at the local pub."

Jasper knew he had all their attention and continued. "See, the joint was rocking, and everybody was dancing and having a good time. Then this attractive girl came up to me and asked if I wanted to dance. I said, why sure. So, the night progressed, and we were having a great time. Even when the slow songs were playing, she got nice and close. She whispered some nothings in my ear, and next thing ya' know we were locking lips and giving each other the tongue."

Marco's eye's opened wide and he nodded his head vigorously. Everyone else was paying close attention with smiles on their faces.

Jasper hushed his voice and continued, "The rest of the night was going simply great and then we found ourselves sitting in my truck. I had my arm wrapped around her shoulder and we were getting hot and heavy. So, I launched my other arm down between her legs and started to get busy. To my utter horror I felt a penis and two balls! Man, I tell you, my woody went limp and I quickly removed my body from her – I mean him. Then I said, "Y'all got to go and I got to go." I pushed this person out of the truck and stepped on the gas and lay awake most of the evening thinking about what happened. I rightly don't think I'll ever be the same."

Everyone started laughing uncontrollably looking at each other and then back to Jasper. Jasper sat back and smiled with confidence knowing he had won their acceptance with that juicy tale.

11

The following days passed without any issues between Jasper and the crew. The summer heat and humidity remained much the same day after day. Finally, some rain arrived, and the crew was forced to find work inside. Jasper felt that it was his job to keep the crew busy. After all, he was somewhat in charge despite what Marco exclaimed. He noticed that Julie was home and Nadia had left early that morning to spend the day with Karl.

Jasper wanted to put some distance between the crew and Julie. So, he came up with a real disgusting job for the guys to do.

The basement of the gatehouse was full of cracked planting pots, bags of old fertilizer, and other odd trash that had collected over the past fifteen years. Most of the stuff had to be loaded and hauled to the dump. This job was the perfect plan to keep everybody far away from the main house.

Jasper jumped in his truck and drove up the hill to the greenhouse. Noticing that everybody's vehicles were parked by the greenhouse, he figured they were all inside staying out of the rain.

Jasper opened the door, and the crew were seated on the counter tops drinking coffee and shoveling sticky buns in their face. King was laying fast asleep on the cement floor. He was soaking wet and the whole room smelled of wet dog and coffee.

An unexcited greeting was muttered from all at once. "Morning, Jasper."

Jasper replied, "Morning to y'all. Say it looks like it's going to rain all day and Mr. Clark wanted me to let you guys know that there's a bunch of stuff in the gatehouse basement that needs to be hauled to the dump. Since there isn't much to do outdoors, now would be a perfect time to take care of this."

Ryan gave Marco a pinched look. Mike and Flint just continued staring at the floor with uninspired looks on their faces.

Marco was the first to speak. He inflated his chest and walked over to Jasper and firmly stated, "Look we have our own program we follow here. Mike and Flint have their responsibilities and Ryan and I planned on cleaning and sharpening the chainsaw blades today – do you understand?" Marco finished curtly.

Jasper stepped back from Marco and raised up his hands, "Listen! I don't rightly understand your so-called, program. All I know is that Ethan asked for me to make sure this project gets completed. You follow me?"

At this point, Mike saw a confrontation brewing and decided to speak up, "Alright, alright, we'll get on it. The kid and I will feed the animals and then we'll meet you guys at the gatehouse."

Since everybody looked up to and respected Mike, they decided to oblige Jasper's request. Marco and Ryan left the greenhouse muttering between themselves while Mike and Flint gathered some brooms and shovels.

King opened his eyes to find the morning meeting was over. He then needed to decide which party he was going to go with. He gave Jasper a quick look and shivered, shook himself dry and proceeded to follow Mike and

Flint.

Foster and Faye had been awake listening to the entire conversation. Foster was lying next to Faye. He quietly stated, "You know that Jasper guy has cleverly sent everybody to the other end of the property."

"What is your point, poppy head." replied Faye.

Foster leaped out of the bed wearing his red union suit pajamas staring at Faye wide-eyed. "Don't you see he's going to make his move on Julie. She's home today, you know."

Faye whipped the covers off her, got up and walked over to their make-shift kitchen. "We'll deal with this problem, after I put some coffee in me. The smell was driving me crazy earlier when the boys came in. Anyway, we have some time, so get yourself dressed, and we'll come up with a plan."

Once Mike and Flint finished feeding the animals, they piled into the golf cart with King to meet the other guys at the gatehouse. Jasper observed this while sitting in the truck and figured now was his chance to pay Julie a visit. Before doing so, Jasper needed to come up with an excuse for coming into the house. He decided to tell Julie that he needed to make a few adjustments to the water heater. This would get him inside and a chance to start a conversation with her.

Jasper rolled his truck down the hill and slowly walked towards the front door. As he walked past the silo-shaped playhouse, he thought he saw a face appear behind the tiny window of the door. Jasper looked again but this time he saw nothing. He quickly dismissed it, but his alien senses told him otherwise. He then walked onto the porch and knocked on the door.

After several moments Julie opened the door with a big smile which she immediately dialed down when she saw who it was. She didn't want to come off rude, so she composed herself and stated, "Oh... Hi Jasper what's up?"

Jasper smiled and replied, "Just needed to check on the house's water heater; mind if I come in?"

Julie stepped back, opened the door, and let him in the hallway. She replied, "Oh sure, do what you need to. I'll be upstairs if you need me."

Jasper paused and attempted to engage Julie with some small talk, "How's school going for you. Have you made any friends?"

Julie was already in motion up the stairs. She froze for a split second to think how she was going to reply, and then turned back towards him. "There are a few friendly people I've met, but it's the beginning of the first semester and I'm very overloaded with homework, which I happen to be way behind on. So sorry to be brief Jasper; I'll catch you later."

Just then Polly darted down the stairs wearing a determined look. Jasper was a bit startled by Polly's abrupt presence and he quickly redirected his focus to the cellar stairs. "Alright Julie, I understand. Listen, with your father gone for a spell, don't hesitate to call if you need anything. Alright?"

Julie looked back at Jasper and thought, maybe this guy was alright. After all, with his wavy-blonde hair and blue eyes he kind of won her over for a second.

At that moment Polly stopped dead in her tracks. She studied the look on Julie's face and then looked up at Jasper. Polly sat down, licked one paw, and wiped her ear. She looked back up at Julie as if to say, "Really, this creep?"

Polly's cleaning activity was abruptly halted when from the corner of her gaze, she saw two fast moving streaks bolt through the slightly opened front door. Polly knew exactly who and what had just come inside. She thought, "What are those two doing in the house?"

Jasper pretended to go about his business. He walked over to the cellar door, turned on the light and started down the stairway. He was slightly miffed by Julie's casual indifference but knew it would take some time to win her over. So, he continued down into to the cellar just to have a look around.

Fay and Foster were standing behind the kitchen door catching their breath. Foster turned and looked out from the crack in the door. He then became frozen by the sight of a grey, furry nose and whiskers.

Polly had found them and wanted to get a few things out in the open. She whispered between the crack. "Alright you two it's time we came face to face once and for all. Don't worry. I'm not going to eat you, but I need to know what you are both up to."

Thinking that this was the end, Foster had both his arms grasped tightly around Faye. He turned and looked into Faye's eyes and realized what a scared mouse he had just turned into.

Faye pealed him off her and brought one of his arms down to her side and held it tightly. Faye whispered loudly, "Alright, we're coming out, but if you try anything funny, we'll blast you into the next dimension – understand?"

Polly tucked her paws underneath her chest and then relaxed in a fur-turkey pose. "Very well. You can come out now," she calmly stated.

Foster nervously rattled off, "You know, we've been meaning to introduce ourselves for quite some time now, but... uh, you know... we thought you might have wanted to eat now and ask questions later if you know what I mean."

Polly stated, "Look – I'm the family cat, both loved and

well-fed by Julie and I don't want anything to get in the way of that. So, tell me. What is your purpose here? I mean, you too have always been hovering around. I thought you were just interested in plants, flowers stuff like that."

Polly then shifted her eyes to Foster; "And especially the poppies for you my good man."

Now more relaxed, Faye calmly replied, "Yes this is all true. We have always loved this family, especially Julie's mother Sarah. She was so in tune with the plants and flowers. As a matter of fact, she would have made a real fine fairy folk if she weren't so tall. We also know that Julie and Ethan both have wonderful talents to offer this world, but the fact of the matter is we have recently discovered that there is another non-human invested in this family."

Polly slowly sat up on her hind legs and cocked her head looking at them. "And who might this other non-human be I ask?"

Foster blurted out, "Why... the serpent named Martin! Surely you must know of this creature. He lives in the water and gets around in other ways – mentally that is. You must have seen him by now?"

Polly peered back at him for a couple seconds, thinking these fairies and their realms are just too much. Slowly she shook her head from side to side. "No, I can't say ever had the pleasure of meeting this fellow. Besides, I don't like water very much thank you."

Faye announced, "Ethan has a significant purpose to fulfill as a teacher of men. Martin has been placed on earth to aid in his development and protection."

Just then a noise came from the bottom of the cellar stairs. It was Jasper on his way back up. This meant it was time for the fairies to exit and to do so quickly.

Foster and Faye looked at each other and made a mad dash out the front door. Their sudden reaction took Polly by surprise, which caused her to back up. She then turned to see Jasper standing at the top of the stairs.

Jasper leaned forward and put his hand out. In a high-pitched voice. He called to Polly, "Here kitty kitty."

Polly remained still and gave Jasper a good stare down but didn't approach him. She looked up and was about to rub his hand and remembered what King had told her. Instead, she quickly ran down the hallway and approached the foot of the stairs, took one more look back and then made a bee line upstairs to Julie's room.

Jasper realized getting close to Julie within the confines of her home wasn't going to work. He thought since Julie didn't have a car, she might want to join him for a ride into town sometime. She might even want to go out some night to see a movie.

Jasper left the house and walked back to his truck. Before leaving he was still curious about what he saw behind the window of the playhouse door. He stood looking at the door and then gazed up at the entire building.

Unseen by Jasper, Foster and Faye had sequestered themselves behind the trunk of a large rhododendron along-side the playhouse.

Jasper approached the front door and peered inside the window. The room was illuminated by a tiny fraction of light coming from a small window near the ceiling. He could see a rocking horse, various dolls, and several low bookshelves. The linoleum floor was decorated with pictures of Nursery Rhyme characters such as Humpty Dumpty, Little Red Riding Hood and Snow White and the Seven Dwarfs. He wanted badly to go inside, but as far as he knew Mike was the only one who had a key.

Now realizing nothing was going on inside, Jasper decided to see how the crew's cleaning project was coming along, so he returned to his truck and drove off to the gatehouse.

Foster grabbed Faye's hand and slowly walked out from

behind the bush. They both looked at each other and back to the door window. Just then, the supposedly locked door opened a crack and from it followed a small blast of stuffy, strange-smelling air. Somewhat shocked, they collected themselves and slowly stepped inside.

No sooner had they made a few feet inside a sweet female voice called out, "Well, hello there my friends. Please come in. My name is Emily. Who are you?"

Emily looked to be a young girl between the age of seven or eight. She had shoulder length curly-blonde hair and wore a one-piece dress. At first, she appeared translucent, but within a few moments her figure changed to a solid form.

Now smiling down at the two fairies, she continued, "I know what you two are... your fairies! I've seen pictures of your kind in my books. Oh, this is wonderful. Tell me what brings you to Woodlands and what are your names?"

Foster remained silent. Faye smiled and in her polite fashion, replied, "Hello, my name is Faye, and this is Foster. We came here with the new family that now lives on the estate."

Emily smiled, "Yes, I know of them. They seem like genuinely nice people. I like King, the dog, too. As a matter of fact, I've seen everyone here, but they can't see me." She chuckled.

Faye softly inquired, "Why are you still here? Don't you want to move on to the next progression of your soul?"

Emily took a seat on a small chair and explained. "When I was alive, my parents didn't have much time to spend with me. So, I created my own little world within this playhouse. Now that I'm a spirit, I can see through the roof, look at the sky and see other planets and dimensions beyond this one. I have my books, dolls and everything that is important to me. You see, fairies, I really love the Woodlands and the grounds. I don't know if you are aware, but there is a dark force living in the pond. Do you know who I mean?"

Faye replied, "Emily, we are aware of this entity. He is parading as a human man named Jasper. We have been informed that he has designs on the owner's daughter, Julie. If you help us defend this family, we promise we will help you cross over when you're ready. However, we must be careful. Neither of us know the limits of his powers."

Emily gave the fairies a big smile and replied, "Your wish is my command, master of the lamp... That's from Aladdin, do you know the story?"

Foster and Faye looked back at Emily with confused looks on their faces and simultaneously shook their heads.

Emily elaborated. "Well, it just happens to be one of my favorite stories, you know. There's this genie that's trapped in a bottle, and..."

Foster interrupted her and whispered loudly, "Emily, I would love to hear more of this genie, but we must go check on Julie, you know, the owner's daughter... to make sure she's alright."

Emily joyfully replied, "Sure, Let's go."

12

It was mid-September, and the daytime temperature was still hovering in the high 80's. A long flatbed truck arrived delivering a huge amount of rolled grass sod. The sod was to be placed near the bath house around the pool, the slate patio and beyond. For it not to dry out, the rolls had to be put down immediately. This meant everybody had to lend a hand, even Jasper.

The morning went by quickly and most of the sod was put in place. This was an especially fast paced and dirty job. Dried mud and tiny bits of green grass were stuck on everyone's face and arms. Everyone's shirts had armpit stains, which gave off a ripe odor when a small but welcome breeze came through.

Marco stood up and flung his trowel into the ground, making it stick upright like a knife. "This shit blows chunks. It's time for lunch and maybe a beer or two."

Ryan replied, "I'm starving and need to get my ass into some shade for a spell."

Mike looked up and wiped his forehead, "Amen to that, but before we do anything, we need to get the sprinklers going on this grass sod. I'll go up to the green house and get'em."

Jasper, who seemed unfazed by the work or the heat, remained on his knees. He glanced around at everybody and said, "I don't think we should stop, and I also don't think drinking beer should be part of the program either."

Marco looked over at Jasper and retorted with a stinging reply, "Don't care what you think, Jasper. We need a break, and we'll drink a beer if we want. Knock yourself out Jasper. Let's go Ryan."

The two gave no more attention to Jasper and began walking to the parking lot. Mike grabbed the wheelbarrow and slowly followed behind them.

The color of Jasper's face began to turn a bright crimson red. Flint was aware of this, and he suddenly stopped what he was doing. He stood up and told Jasper he was going into the bath house to take a leak.

Jasper shook his head, feeling frustrated that he couldn't maintain any authority over guys, especially Marco. He began to feel rage and found it hard to retain his false appearance. Jasper decided he had better duck away to his watery sanctuary to rejuvenate.

With everybody gone Flint saw this as an opportunity to grab his guitar and record a few tracks on Mr. Clark's fancy reel-to-reel. He downed a large glass of water, grabbed his twelve-string guitar, and got busy.

Once Flint figured out how to work the machine, he pressed record and proceeded to play one original piece after another. The high ceiling and terracotta tile floor gave the guitar a huge reverb effect which inspired Flint to no end. He proceeded to use most of his lunch hour to record.

◆ ◆ ◆

A little while later, Marco and Ryan returned from town

with several quarts of beer and some sandwiches. Since Jasper was nowhere to be seen, they all sat Indian-style and passed a healthy marijuana joint around.

Ryan started in with one of his long-winded stories about a carpenter that used to spend most of his paycheck every Friday on the horses. He closed the tale explaining how the carpenter 's wife was so fed up with his irresponsibility, that one morning she decided to take a crap on his chest before he woke up. This got Marco's attention, and everybody responded with, "Oh my god... Holy shit!"

Marco gave Ryan a light punch on the arm and said, "Sure you're not the carpenter in this story?"

Ryan punched Marco back, although a bit harder, and exclaimed, "Fuck you."

It was on this note that Jasper appeared back on scene. This broke up the pow-wow. Everybody went back to work and then finished out the rest day and was exhausted.

Fortunately, it was Friday, and the crew had the whole weekend to rest up and enjoy their paychecks.

On their way home they make a quick stop at a local gorge. This gave them a chance to wash off all the mud and grass that had become glued to every exposed part of their skin.

After a few jumps in the water, the three then sat at the edge of the gorge and shared their dissatisfaction with Jasper.

Marco cursed him and said how he wasn't going to take any more orders from him.

Ryan explained, "If he worked for the county, those guys would have tied two cinder blocks to his legs and thrown him in the river by now."

Flint interjected, "We need to have Mike ask Ethan to get him off our backs. We know what to do, and we work our asses off. That creature has no business telling us how to do our jobs."

Ryan chimed in, "Oh, he's a creature alright. I can't quite figure him out, and I've worked with all kinds of fellas. He's definitely a strange bird."

Marco spit on the ground and said, "He's shit."

13

The interior of the bath house was now finished. It was early Saturday morning, and Nadia had just finished mopping the entire floor. Julie was on her way down to check out the pool and listen to the new sound system. She arrived, opened the door, and was taken back by the beauty of the finished decor.

Nadia leaned the mop against the wall, and said to Julie, "It's beautiful, isn't it'?

Julie replied, "This is so awesome! Nadia, why don't you go get your bathing suit on and we'll take a dip in the pool."

"Yes, I feel so sticky and sweaty; I'll be right back," she exclaimed.

Julie walked over to the sound system cabinet and opened the louvered doors. She turned on the receiver and dialed in the local radio station which happened to be playing Aerosmith's "Sweet Emotion".

She proceeded to slowly increase the volume until the music filled the entire space. Julie closed her eyes and reveled in the high-fidelity bliss. The song soon ended and was followed by loud and obnoxious commercials.

Julie then switched the dial to the reel to reel. The only music that had been recorded on the blank reel was Flint's twelve-string guitar music. After a few scrapping noises and some strings being tuned, the walls started pumping out a small orchestra of guitar music.

Julie listened intently as the melodic chords and strumming captured her attention. She thought it sounded somewhat familiar, but knew it wasn't any artist she had listened to before. Letting the player continue, Julie went back to the changing room and slipped into her bathing suit.

Nadia was now suited and jumping on the diving board. She then executed a perfect swan dive into the pool. Julie just ran and jumped into the deep end, splashing water everywhere.

The two enjoyed making some laps back and forth and then relaxed in the lounge chairs on the blue-stone patio. The music stopped, and Nadia asked, "Who was playing that interesting guitar music?"

Julie replied, "I'm not quite sure, but it sounded like that worker who plays his guitar in the parking lot every once in a while."

Nadia agreed, "Yes... yes it does. Oh, what is his name, the young boy with the long hair? Let's see, Mike calls him The Kid, but I believe his name is Flint. He's about your age, Julie, and kind of cute too. Maybe you should talk to him and tell him what you think about his recording. It's time for you to start making some friends other than just your schoolmates – no?"

Julie gave the idea some thought and agreed. "You're right, Nadia. I'm going to introduce myself next week. You know Jasper asked me if I wanted to take a ride into town with him. I thought that maybe I would. Besides, I'd like to check out some of the local shops. By the way, what do you make of Jasper?"

Nadia didn't think long at all. She waved her hand to the side of her face and said, "I've only passed him a few times when I was leaving with Karl. He is handsome, I guess, but not really my type. Why do you ask? I didn't figure you to go for older men. I mean he's not old, just older – you know."

Julie smiled and shook her head, "No no, I'm not interested in Jasper. There's something about him, like maybe I've met the guy before, but that's impossible. He's from Oklahoma, and this is my first time in the states."

Nadia reached over and gently touched Julie's hand, "Relax, dear, I think with your father away right now everything seems more foreign. I like this place, and especially my new friend Karl. Yet there was something special about the old house in England. I guess because your mother's spirit was so present there. After all, she put so much into all the flowers and plantings. Oh dear, I'm sorry. We are here now, so let's enjoy another dip in this wonderful swimming pool – alright?"

Julie smiled and nodded her head and then they both flung themselves back into the pool.

Later that afternoon Jasper walked up to the main house and knocked on the door. Several moments passed before Julie answered. She opened the door, "Hey Jasper, how are you, what's up?"

Jasper gave a big grin and replied, "I'm taking that ride into town now and was wondering if you wanted to tag along. Thought you might need a few things or just want to get out of the house."

Julie replied, "You know, I could use a break. Give me a couple minutes and I'll be right out."

Polly was busy munching on some cat kibble in the corner of the kitchen. She glanced up to Julie and gave her a look, as if to say, "Really?" Knowing she was unable to communicate to her, Polly returned to chowing on her kibble.

"No problem," Jasper stated with a grin. "I'll be in the truck."

Before he climbed into the truck, Jasper peeked over in

the direction of the playhouse. He stopped momentarily to see if he could pick up on the same vibe he encountered before.

Jasper was about to try the door again when Julie came bursting out the front door. She jangled the keys, locked the door, and loudly stated, "I'm ready; let's go!"

Jasper replied, "Y'all, ready to roll. I'm ready – let's roll."

During the short ride to the village Jasper made sure not to come on too strong or ask any prying questions. The two chatted about Nadia and Karl and agreed their relationship was getting hot and heavy. In between several short conversations Julie spent most of the ride just staring out the window.

Jasper parked the truck on the main drag, and then turned to Julie and said, "There's a soft serve ice cream joint right across the street. Why don't you do your thing, and we meet there in an hour. How does that sound?"

Julie replied, "Oh... alright, yes that sounds perfect. I didn't think you would be interested in checking out the dress shop with me."

Jasper laughed and replied, "Yeah, you got that right. I've got some stuff to get at the hardware store, so you go do your program and I'll do mine. I'll see you later."

The two divided, and after the hour had passed, they both convened back at the ice cream shop. It was a sunny day, and the temperature was above eighty, so a nice cold ice cream was just the thing.

They both got their order and sat at one of the small bistro tables in front of the shop. Jasper was being a perfect gentleman. It seemed to him that he was beginning to win Julie's trust. He wiped his mouth with his napkin and said, "Nothing like the enjoyment of a cold ice cream on a hot summer's day." He then made a couple funny remarks about some of the locals passing by. They both laughed, and then walked back to the truck.

On the ride back, Julie finally felt relaxed and was glad to have checked out the downtown. Up until now she only had been at home, on the train and in school. She was still a bit unsure about Jasper but enjoyed his Oklahoman manor along with his humorous observations. She found Jasper to be good looking, but she couldn't get Nadia's statement out of her head about him being an older man.

Julie then thought about the workers on the estate and how they were all handsome in their own way. Marco was strong and always had his shirt opened with the sleeves ripped off. Ryan had the Braveheart thing going on, but Flint was cute and played this beautiful guitar music. After this brief assessment she reminded herself to make friends with Flint.

At the same time Jasper was pondering how good things were going. He was finally making some headway thinking today's triumph gave him the confidence that everything might just go as planned.

Both were off in their own heads as the truck rolled in front of the main house. Jasper tipped his aviation mirror sunglasses down his nose and turned to Julie. "I don't know about you, but that ice cream made my day."

Julie was somewhat startled from being deep in her own thoughts, but then she turned to him, "Oh, yeah, that was grand. We should do this again." She jumped out of the truck, waved goodbye and walked into the house.

Jasper smiled at her with one of his crescent-moon smiles. He pushed his sunglasses back up and drove back to the gatehouse with his frog-like eyes gleaming.

14

Monday morning had arrived. Ryan's car flew past the gatehouse with hard-rock music blasting from the open car windows. At that moment Nadia and Julie were getting into the car to leave for the train station. Ryan slowed the car down and made the turn past the main house. Marco grinned at Nadia after noticing the tight sweater she was wearing. Flint made eye contact with Julie and she returned with a friendly smile.

◆ ◆ ◆

Moments before, the blasting music had awakened Jasper sleeping in the gatehouse. He climbed out of bed and sluggishly made his way to the bathroom. The need to become immersed in water was much needed. Jasper was used to spending days in his watery layer, and the absence was starting to take its toll.

Jasper was now fully dressed, he walked out of the gatehouse feeling confident, refreshed, and ready to implement his next move. It was at this time Nadia and Julie approached the gatehouse on their way to the train station.

Jasper affixed his aviator shades and put on his cowboy

hat. Both girls smiled and waved at him. Jasper tipped his hat in the manor of a gentleman cowboy of the old west.

In order not to miss the morning train, the girls kept going. Nadia exited out of the driveway and accelerated onto the main road.

Julie blurted out, "I went downtown with Jasper last night. We both ran some errands and had some ice cream afterwards."

Nadia turned to her quickly and gave her an eagle-eyed stare. "Really, honey, you hardly know this guy. With your father away right now, you should have asked me. I would have taken you."

Julie rolled her eyes, "Thanks for the offer Nadia, but it was fine. He's not a bad guy. He is no doubt different, but he's kind of cute, in a foreign sort of way – at least to me. I mean he's nothing like your regular British man you know; I find his accent a gas."

Nadia nodded but kept her eyes on the road, "Still Julie, I think you should be making friends with some of your schoolmates. What about that young man Flint? I thought you said you were going to introduce yourself to him."

Julie's cheeks began to turn red and she smiled. "Yes, I still plan to. I also want to let him know how much I enjoyed his recording."

Nadia nodded two times slowly, she smiled and turned to Julie. "Yes, you should."

Nadia and Julie giggled when their attention was abruptly switched to the news announcement on the car radio.

The news reporter spoke with a serious tone in his voice. *"This morning in England two bombs went off. One in Regent's Park, the other in Hyde Park. Eleven members of the household cavalry and the Royal Green Jackets were killed. Sadly, seven horses were also killed.* The announcer finished saying, *"Security has been issued throughout the city, and es-*

pecially at all the major airports."

Both girls were momentarily dumbfounded by this disturbing news. Julie blurted out, "Oh my god – airports! Nadia, when is Dad coming back?"

Nadia touched the top of Julie's hand. "Oh, honey he's not due back for a couple more weeks. Don't worry I'm sure they'll get to the bottom of this before he and your grandparents come back. The authorities will catch these guys and put them behind bars where they belong. Now relax. These kinds of things used to happen in my country every other week."

Shortly, they arrived in front of the train station. Nadia turned to Julie and calmly spoke. "You relax and keep your eyes open today. I'll see you later. Please don't worry yourself; all will be fine."

Julie stepped out of the station wagon, turned, and gave Nadia a reluctant smile. "Yes, alright. I'll see you later."

Back at the estate, Mike and King were sitting in the golf cart parked at the top of the hill by the greenhouse. The three guys remained in Ryan's car with the windows rolled down. Just at that moment Jasper rounded the corner in his truck. The three guys climbed out of Ryan's car and stretched, preparing themselves for another long, hot day. The lawns needed mowing and weed-whacking. Since there was plenty of property to cover, this was going to be an all-day project.

Jasper climbed out of his truck, stood in one spot, and then looked Marco up and down, giving him a nasty stink eye.

Marco glanced up and took notice of the look on Jasper's face. He then made direct eye contact with Jasper and leaned forward toward him. "What the fuck is your problem?"

Jasper took a step back, "Hold on there, Com-padre. That's no way to greet the boss."

Marco launched into a tirade, "First of all you're not my boss. Second, what was that look you gave me?"

Jasper figured he better deflate this situation. "Alright, alright I don't want to argue with y'all, but this is a place of employment – not a rock concert. I really don't think Mr. Clark would appreciate you smoking the peace-pipe before coming to work, do you?"

Marco gave Jasper a smug look and said, "First of all we've got three minutes before we clock in. What I do on my own time is my business. Second, I can do any job on this estate straight or stoned. This stuff isn't rocket science we're doing here."

Jasper realized it was a waste of time arguing with Marco, so he calmly asked, "What's your program today, because I think it would be a good idea to mow the grass."

Marco was not only hung over from too many beers the night before, but he was now losing his wake n' bake buzz. "Way ahead of you Jasper. Like I said, we know what needs to be done around here. We've have been doing it long before you arrived."

"I copy that." Jasper replied. "It's my job to know what's going on around here and that's all I'm doing so you have yourself a nice day."

The morning flew by and It was now lunch time and the temperature had risen into the 90's. Ryan and Marco had left to pick up sandwiches from the downtown deli. This allowed some time for Mike and Flint catch up on things. The two of them were both situated underneath a huge weeping willow tree that bordered the pond. The shade and the light breeze felt good after the morning hustle.

Unbeknownst to Mike and Flint, Faye and Foster were

nestled way atop the willow tree in an abandoned squirrel's nest. They had wanted to speak privately with Mike to find out from him how things were progressing between Julie and Flint, but Foster and Faye knew Flint wasn't ready to meet them yet, so instead, they sat and listened quietly.

Mike took a seat against the tree and fired up one of his *Pall Malls*. He motioned to Flint to come over and said, "Sit down and take a load off kid."

Flint smiled back, and then plopped himself down laying completely flat on the grass.

Mike commented on the heat and slapped a mosquito on his forearm and asked, "So kid, what's new with you?"

Flint ecstatically replied, "Well, I'm getting my own car this coming weekend. I managed to save up enough money to buy this old Chevy Impala. She's not much to look at, but everything else seems fine with it."

Mike replied, "That's great kid. Maybe you can start taking some girls out. Does the car still have a back seat?"

Flint grinned. "Oh yeah, that's probably in better shape than the rest of the car."

Being careful not to sound like he was prying, Mike asked, "Have you got any sweethearts you plan to go cruising with?"

Flint felt a bit embarrassed to reply that he didn't. "No, but I'm thinking about asking the boss's daughter out. You know, I'll see if she would like to go hiking or something."

Mike smiled back, thinking to himself that this was going easier than he had planned. "Yeah, Julie's real pretty. I'll bet she'll say yes for sure."

Flint raised his eyebrows in surprise. "You think so Mike? You believe I've got a chance with her? I mean, she's wealthy and I'm just a simple, working stiff."

Mike looked Flint in the eye, "Listen, kid, it's what you have inside that's important. You've got talent and class and in my book that's a winning combination. Don't put yourself down. When you see her again, just come right out and ask her, I mean, after you get through some of the small talk first."

Flint replied with an excited, but nervous, tone in his voice. "Right, I get what you mean."

Fay and Foster looked at each other and raised their arms to give a silent high-five. They now knew things were about to unfold and go as planned.

Later that afternoon, Flint was relaxing in the greenhouse with a glass of water. King was laying on the cement floor, absorbing the coolness it offered. Polly appeared through the open door, which got Flint's attention. Flint loved all animals and especially cats. He started petting Polly and she soaked it up, switching back and forth against his hands.

Four o'clock had rolled around, and Julie was now already back from school. She decided to walk up the hill to look at the plants inside the greenhouse. There was a bird of paradise plant that was practically the size of a small tree. Julie remembered seeing the plant when she first arrived and wanted to admire its blossoms.

Flint was in a furry bliss with Polly when Julie walked in. She interrupted them commenting, "I see you've found a friend?"

Flint quickly turned his head in surprise. "Oh, hi... I was just taking a break from the outside heat."

Flint was nervous, but he rallied quickly to introduce himself, "Hi I'm Flint. You're Julie, right? We've seen each other in passing, but it's nice to finally meet you."

Julie leaned against the counter while Polly started rubbing against her back. "Yes, it's nice to meet you too. You know, I've been meaning to tell you how much I enjoyed listening to your recording. Interesting stuff! You're exceptionally good."

Flint bashfully replied, "Oh really... wow... thanks, it's just some stuff I made up. Glad you enjoyed it."

Julie continued. "I've also heard you playing in the parking lot a couple times. My father is a musician also. He plays the piano. I'm afraid I don't play an instrument, but I can appreciate the work it takes to create music. Instead, I draw designs for clothing, mostly for women. That's what I'm studying in New York – fashion design that is." She quickly shifted her attention to the other side of the room. "I came up to see the flowers on the bird of paradise plant. It's such a cool and interesting plant."

Flint turned his attention to the glassed-in portion of the greenhouse and moved toward the plant. "Yeah, it looks like something from another planet – very awesome plant."

They both stood in front of the plant and admired its beauty. Julie spoke up, "You know my mother knew everything about plants, shrubs and trees. She was quite amazing."

Flint looked back at her with a serious look. "You say, she was?"

Julie removed some of the shriveled dead leaves off the base of the plant and gave Flint a quick glance then replied, "Yes, she passed away several years ago. That's why my father thought it would be best to move somewhere else. You know, put the past behind us and try to move on. So here we are."

Flint glanced back. "So sorry to hear about your

mother, Julie. Do like it here?"

Julie snapped out of her funk and replied, "Oh yes, very much so. This place is nice. I love the trees, the buildings, and the grounds. Guess I'm pretty much a nature girl. The place we lived in England was much smaller but somewhat like this."

This was Flint's opportunity to make a date and he knew it was now or never. "Say, Julie, I love nature too and especially hiking in the mountains. I grew up about sixty miles north of here, and one of my favorite places to hike is a trail called, "The *Lemon Squeeze*". It's a cool, rocky trail, located on the property of the *Mohonk Mountain* reserve in *New Paltz, New York*. I'm getting my own car this weekend and thought maybe you'd like to come along and check it out. So, maybe we could go the following weekend. How does that sound to you?

Julie had no fear of Flint and decided to reply with an ecstatic, "Yes, that sounds wonderful."

Flint was thrilled but realized he had been slacking for a good half hour. "Julie, that's great! I'll talk to you next week about it, but I better get back to work."

Excited and a bit tongue-tied, Flint gave Polly one more pet, smiled back at Julie, and left the greenhouse.

Back in England Ethan lay awake looking out the window of Ian's guest room. Ethan wondered how Julie was doing and if Jasper was working out. From downstairs he could hear the faint sound of the television news. The announcer's voice had a serious tone. Ethan heard the mention of bombs, airports, and terrorists. This prompted him to get up and go downstairs to find out what had happened.

Ethan entered the kitchen and saw Ian glued to a small portable television. Ian turned to Ethan with a blank stare and shook his head. "Man, this isn't good. There have been several bombings right here in England. Security has also been heightened, especially in airports."

Ethan took a seat at the table and listened to the recap of the report. He rubbed his forehead as he digested this alarming news.

Ian was aware of what must be going through Ethan's mind. He walked over and sat down at the table with him.

Ian looked Ethan in the eye and said, "I've been watching this report all morning and I don't think you need to worry. The authorities have this under control, and business should resume. Relax have some coffee and something to eat."

Ethan exhaled a long breath through his lips, "Alright, I guess so."

Ian asked, "When are you supposed to fly back? In a couple weeks, right?"

Now somewhat regrouped, Ethan replied, "Yes in two weeks. I plan to pick up Eric and Victoria on my way to the airport."

At that moment, the idea crossed Ethan's mind that it might be better to put them on an earlier flight if possible. After all, they had already sold their flat in England, and should the situation escalate, they would be safe in the states. Ethan also felt it would be better to have Julie's grandparents at the estate with her. This plan would allow him to still give Ian a hand with his new kitchen project and not to worry so much.

Ian opened the kitchen cabinet and pulled out a box of *Captain Crunch*. Holding it up with a big smile he said, "Now I know this stuff isn't good for you, but it's bound to give you the right amount of sugar buzz to snap you out of your funk. I know you're particularly good about what you eat, but times like these call for drastic measures. So, let's indulge my good man."

Ethan laughed then grabbed the box and popped a few

pieces into his mouth, "You know, this stuff is good."

Now wearing a devilish grin on his face, Ian replied, "Wait until you mix it with milk. I guarantee you'll want to have two bowls of this stuff."

A little later that afternoon Ethan was able to switch flights so the grandparents could fly out the following day. He also contacted Nadia to have her and Julie plan to meet and pick them up at the airport.

15

The heat wave had finally lifted, ushering in cooler and more comfortable weather. Jasper returned from the mailbox at the front of the driveway and realized It was time for him to communicate and report back to the superiors. Jasper parked his truck at the gatehouse, and then walked to the stone bridge at the north end of the pond.

Once he arrived, Jasper reverted to a bullfrog and jumped into the water. He swam down to a large round rock located at the base of the stone bridge. From the center of his forehead, he began to project a green light at the rock. Within a few minutes the rock appeared soft and rippled. He then proceeded through the opening and arrived at the other end.

Now in his own dimension, Jasper hopped onto a nearby flat rock. Before him lay a pathway of more flat rocks that led to a half dozen domed building structures in the distance.

On either side of the path was an expansive body of shallow water stretching miles in each direction. The sky was greenish blue, dotted with what appeared to be many brightly lit stars. The air was extremely dense and slightly humid. There was no visible sun, but light filled the cloudless sky.

Jasper then morphed into a six-foot-tall human with arms and legs. His head grew in proportion to his body but remained that of a frog's. He drew in a deep breath and was comforted by the sights, sounds and atmosphere of his own home.

Slowly he moved forward on the stone pathway towards the structures that lay in the distance. It was time to present his information and request his desire to bring the earth girl back with him. It wouldn't be until the next full moon that the vortex between the two worlds would close forever.

Jasper finally approached the main structure and walked in. Immediately two other creatures that resembled himself stopped him. One of the creatures quietly said, "Wait here Jasper, I will inform the elders that you have arrived."

The one guard stayed with Jasper while the other went behind a large curtain. He then returned and motioned for Jasper to come forward. "They will see you now."

Behind the curtain seated at a table were three more creatures resembling Jasper. One appeared to be much older and wore a glowing amulet on a chain around its neck. This one looked directly into Jasper's eyes, which placed him in a trance-like state.

As Jasper stood motionless, the elder was able to view Jasper's thoughts and experiences. This process revealed all information, and no lies could be told.

After several minutes Jasper was free of the elder's scan. The same elder turned and whispered to one of the other for several moments. With a dissatisfied look on his face the head elder returned his gaze, "Jasper you have done quite well gathering the information we requested and since you have fulfilled your duty, we will allow you to come back very shortly. However, your interest in bringing this female back to our dimension is not recommended."

He continued. "Let me ask – is this earth girl willing to come back with you? Does she know who and what you are? If so, then I cannot stop you. However, if you invite unwanted guests into our realm, your actions will result in extreme discipline. Do I make myself clear, Jasper?"

Since Jasper couldn't honestly answer any of these questions he simply replied, "I understand, and will do as you request."

The head elder waved his hand across his face. "We are finished here; you may return. I suggest you give much thought to what we've discussed. You have made mistakes in the past and therefore you have been sentenced to this earth realm. I trust you won't disobey us again."

The two elders then stood from the table and walked behind another curtain, leaving Jasper to contemplate his decision.

On his walk back to portal Jasper digested the elder's warning, which made him feel rather uneasy and unsure on how to proceed. His desire to have Julie was strong, but he also couldn't bear the thought of returning for another assignment. Jasper's needs outweighed any directive from the elder. Therefore, he was determined to bring Julie back – one way or another.

Later that afternoon Nadia and Julie left to pick up her grandparents at the airport. Their plane arrived on time and warm hugs were exchanged by all. Julie was very much looking forward to having her grandmother Victoria around again.

Victoria Clark had long gray hair that she wore tied back in a ponytail. She had an almond-shaped face with big blue eyes. Her eyebrows were very pronounced, which amplified her intense gaze. Victoria was well-educated and came from a very affluent British family. However, despite her rigid and formal demeanor, she was still a very down-to-earth person.

Eric Clark was a stocky, muscular Scottish man with a big white beard and mustache. If you dressed him in a red cap with small wire framed glasses, he could pass for Santa Claus. Eric had been a plumber for thirty years and was now retired, but he had the stamina of a forty-year-old man. He was a bit old-fashioned but being a trades-man instilled him with a deep appreciation for the common man.

The ride home was filled with stories, memories, and a detailed description of the estate and all the people that worked there. Eric enjoyed hearing about the workers and the new bath house.

Victoria expressed her reservations about moving to the states, but she was excited to get busy decorating and working in the gardens.

The time flew by, and they finally arrived at the drive-way of the Estate. Eric and Victoria were immediately impressed and felt relieved to be in an environment to which they were more accustomed.

Currently, Jasper was still busy rejuvenating himself under the bridge. He was aware of the station wagon roll-ing over, so he prepared himself to meet the new arrivals.

Nadia stopped the station wagon in front of the main house, and everyone got out.

Victoria immediately surveyed the front porch and turned to Julie, "We must get some large, moss-filled hanging planters to line the porch with."

Nadia followed with, "Yes, my boyfriend Karl knows of a local nursery that has such things."

Julie replied, "Of course, and we should do the same for the bath house. Wait until you see this structure; it looks like a Roman temple."

After taking a tour of the main house, everyone made their way down the slate path to the bath house. They walked around the front and then entered inside.

In short time all were engaged in conversation. All the chatter halted when Jasper entered in from the side door. He smiled at everyone and introduced himself. His hair was neatly combed, and he was dressed in smart-looking, casual attire. He dialed up the charm with Victoria by kissing her hand as if she were royalty. He then gave Eric a strong manly handshake. Eric returned the same and winked. Julie was all smiles, which fueled Jasper's desires to no end.

They engaged in separate conversations that echoed throughout the bath house. King had managed to slip inside as well. He watched Jasper and paid close attention to how he was eyeing Julie. Victoria had also been observing how Jasper was admiring Julie. After all, this is what grandmothers do. She found Jasper particularly good looking, but she wasn't used to his southern demeanor.

Victoria found him charming but somewhat of a hillbilly. She then reminded herself that this was just a stigma that television had attached to people with southern accents.

After briefly studying Jasper, Victoria re-entered the conversation that Nadia and Julie were having about wallpaper and various fabrics from around the world.

Eric was happy to be engaged in a conversation with another male, especially after the hour-long drive from the airport with three women. Jasper was giving Eric his full attention as he listened to one of Eric's plumbing nightmare stories.

Fifteen minutes had passed, and it was time to get Victoria and Eric settled into the cabin.

Jasper graciously shook their hands again and made the

comment that he needed to leave to pick up a few things in town. He reached down and patted King on the head and then exited the bath house.

Once Jasper was well out of view, Victoria turned to Julie, "Well, he's an interesting chap. I'm not sure what to make of him. Although I do think he's rather handsome – don't you think Julie?"

Victoria was testing Julie to see how she would react to the question. The smile on Nadia's face quickly dissipated as she waited to hear Julie's response.

Julie's eyes rolled momentarily, and she smiled back at Victoria. "Well, yes, but he's a little too old for me. You know, I'm kind of sweet on one of the young workers here on the estate. His name is Flint, and he plays this remarkably interesting and wonderful guitar music."

Nadia smiled again and shook her head then glanced back at Victoria. Eric continued to smile at Julie.

Victoria was quick to reply, "Oh really? Well, that sounds nice, but does this young man just work on the estate, or is he attending a college nearby?"

Julie's smile diminished from her face. "No, he works on the estate full time; he wants to be a musician."

Eric's expression changed as he darted at look at Victoria. Victoria then decided to change the subject. "So, tell me how are your classes going? Better yet, why don't you tell me all about them at breakfast tomorrow morning."

Nadia sensed Julie's deflation and interjected with an exciting tone in her voice, "Yes, I'll make everybody their own special omelet. We also have these delicious bagels from the city; they are simply wonderful."

Eric and Victoria were then driven to the cabin. Jet lag was setting in, and they were very much in need of some sleep. Their belongings were due to arrive in several days, but the cabin was furnished with the basics.

❖ ❖ ❖

Sunday morning arrived and everyone enjoyed Nadia's omelets. The rest of the day was spent exploring the entire estate.

Since it was the weekend, none of the workers were around except Jasper. He remained in the gatehouse, not wanting to intrude on the family. Instead, he contemplated how he was going to navigate the new arrivals – especially one very observant and inquisitive grandmother.

Jasper realized that this could be a challenge but also figured he could use Victoria's scrutiny to his advantage. Jasper knew once Julie's grandparents met the work crew, he would outshine them all with his refined and adult disposition.

16

Flint arrived Monday morning driving his new car. Following him were Mike, Ryan, and Marco. Everyone parked and walked over to inspect Flint's new ride. Marco gave the tires the old-fashioned kick on the side. Mike congratulated him on his first car. Ryan popped open the hood, and then gave Flint a nod of approval.

The moment was interrupted by the approaching sound of Jasper's truck pulling into the parking lot. Everyone's attention was broken as they turned to give Jasper the usual cold blank look.

Jasper turned the engine off and remained seated in his truck. He rolled down the window and gave everyone a big wide grin. "Jesus! Y'all look like you just ate some bad rabbit or something."

Jasper then turned his attention to Flint's new car. "Look who's fast becoming a real man with his own ride. Congratulations! Hope she serves you well. It doesn't  look like much, but as long as it rolls who cares – right?"

Mike chimed in. "Alright chief, what's the program today? I understand we have some new guests staying in the cabin?"

Jasper stepped out of the truck and motioned for everyone to come into a huddle. "Now Mr. Clark's parents have arrived. I've met them both and they seem like real nice folks. I'd appreciate y'all to be nice, and most importantly watch your language when they're about."

Marco rolled his eyes but didn't say anything. Mike shook his head in agreement.

Jasper continued. "Ethan said to let them join in and help out if they want. After all, they're going to be living here permanently now. You guys will really like Eric, he's a retired plumber and a real hoot. Victoria, on the other hand, seems like she plans on doing her own thing with plants, gardening, and stuff. Mike and Flint, you'll probably end up dealing with her the most."

Jasper continued. "If y'all don't have any program today, I suggest we get the storm glass windows out of the gatehouse. You know, give'em a good wash and get them ready for the main house. After all, the nights are going to start getting cooler. So that's all I got for you guys today. Let's get busy and make a good impression... alright?"

The group disbanded, leaving Jasper standing next to his truck alone. He put his shades back on, climbed back into the truck, and took off for downtown.

Mike and Flint went inside the greenhouse to gather some tools. At that moment, the door opened and in walked Victoria. She was wearing her full gardening regalia with bonnet, apron, and rubber boots.

Both Mike and Flint stepped together before Victoria and introduced themselves. She gave them both a good look up and down. "Nice to meet you. Julie has filled me in on you both. Mike, I understand you've been part of this estate for a while now. I have so many questions for you, but not right now."

Mike smiled back, and nodded, "Be glad to help, and welcome to the Woodlands."

Victoria then turned her attention to Flint. "I under-stand you're quite the guitar player. Did you study under someone?"

Flint, now feeling a bit pressured, quickly relaxed, and replied, "My parents started me with Classical guitar lessons from an old Russian man who was personal friends with Segovia."

Victoria's eyes opened wide. "Oh my, Segovia. Why he's the best, right? Extremely fortunate for you. I would like to hear you play sometime. You know Ethan studied classical piano, and he plays beautifully."

"Yes, Julie mentioned that to me." replied Flint.

Mike could sense Flint's discomfort, so he interjected. "Well, it certainly was a pleasure to meet you. Please let us know if you need our help, and we'll be glad to assist. We better get busy with our duties for the day. I'll be available to answer any questions before I leave today, alright?"

Victoria replied, "That would be lovely; this place is truly remarkable."

Ryan and Marco had already arrived at gatehouse garage and started loading the storm windows into the trailer. Marco was going on about what he would do to the terrorists if he were sent over, and with gusto, stated, "I would hang those bastard's upside down by their balls, and piss in their mouth. I hate those sons-a-bitches."

Ryan was about to elaborate but held his tongue when he saw Eric and King sitting in the golf cart. Eric had been listening to their conversation but didn't interrupt them.

Ryan tapped Marco on the shoulder a couple times to halt him from continuing. He then graciously approached Eric with an outstretched hand.

Eric had a wide smile on his face as he stepped out of the

golf cart. "Hello, pleased to meet you guys, my name is, Eric."

Ryan liked this guy already, "My name is Ryan, and this big mouth over here is Marco."

Marco wiped his hands on his pants and approached Eric. He gave him a strong, aggressive handshake. "I apologize for my language, sir, but these creeps really piss me off."

Eric shook his head slowly. "No need to apologize son, I hate those mother-fuckers too, and I think they should mind their own business."

Ryan looked at Marco, and then they smiled at Eric. They both realized that this relationship was already off to good start.

Eric asked if he could give them a hand. Marco replied, "The more the merrier – nice of you to offer – unlike Jasper, who only manages to give us orders and leaves."

Eric replied, "I take it you aren't too crazy about this guy. I chatted with him yesterday, and he seemed like a good egg. A little odd though; I'll give you that. He strikes me as someone stuck on himself, and maybe a little power hungry."

Ryan shook his head. "You got it, Eric. I know the type well. When I used to work for the county, those guys were a dime a dozen. Eventually, they realize that they're only a big fish in a little pond, or they end up in the pond, if you get my drift." All three laughed and continued the task.

Ryan then heard a motor noise from over his shoulder and turned around. "Well, speak of the devil; here's Jasper now – back from his morning, downtown excursion."

Jasper saw that Eric was pitching in and stopped his truck. "Good morning, Eric. Hope these guys aren't giving you any trouble? Thanks for helping. Tell ya' what, I'll go set up some ladders so we can take down the screens on the main house. See you guys up there."

Jasper knew he better do his part. At the same time,

this also insured that he would be around the main house when Julie came home.

The rest of the morning went smoothly, and everyone was on their best behavior. Victoria eventually joined the crew and approached Jasper to see if he could take her to the nursery later. She also mentioned to him that she wanted to bring Julie along with them for help and advice.

Jasper grinned. "Well, I'd be glad to take y'all. It's only about ten minutes from here." He couldn't have been more pleased by this request.

A few hours later, Julie and Nadia arrived home. They were both excited to see all the activity going on, especially everyone outside working together. Victoria walked over to Julie and gave her a warm embrace. "Welcome home dear. What a beautiful day! Listen, Jasper has offered to take us to the nursery. I want you to come along to help me pick out some hanging baskets. How does that sound?" Julie immediately agreed to go.

Both Jasper and Flint were keenly aware of Julie's arrival, and made a concerted effort to make eye contact with her. Julie turned from her grandmother and chose to lock eyes with Flint first. They both gave each other a brief wave.

Wanting to make a good impression before the owner's in-laws, Flint remained focused on his task. Jasper was aware of their brief exchange and was put off by this. He had no idea they had become acquainted with each other. Jasper's blood boiled, but he knew Flint didn't have a chance with a wealthy girl with a dominating grandmother. He then approached Julie and Victoria. "Whenever you guys want to take that ride, just let me know. Hi Julie. How did your day go?"

Julie smiled back, "Oh, you know, just another day. Mondays always seem to drag. I'm going to change and get ready; see you guys shortly."

Within a short time, Julie came bursting out the front door of the main house. Victoria was already seated in the wicker couch on the porch. She waived her hands to get Jasper's attention, and called out, "Hello, Jasper! We're ready to go!"

The three climbed into the truck with Julie seated in between Jasper and Victoria. Mike and Flint stepped out of the way of the approaching truck and gave a quick wave. Mike looked at them, thinking to himself; "What do we have here?"

Flint felt a bit unnerved but resigned that there was nothing he could do in this situation.

Jasper was happy as a clam to have Julie sitting close to him. The smell of her perfume and her long hair brushing against his arm was driving him crazy.

Later, when the three returned from the nursery, it was apparent that everyone had left for the day, and the sun was about to set. Jasper dropped Julie and Victoria off at the main house. "Well, good night ladies. I'll go hang these plants in the greenhouse and have the guys water them in the morning."

Victoria graciously replied, "Jasper, thanks for all your help, and also allowing us the time to make up our minds."

Jasper replied, "Anytime you need a ride – you let me know. I also mentioned to Julie that there's a little movie theater downtown. If you're up for it, we can all go check a flick out some night. How does that sound?"

Victoria quickly looked at Julie and nodded to Jasper. "Well, that would be nice. We'll let you know; good night now."

Jasper couldn't stop thinking of the look on Julie's face when she saw Flint earlier that afternoon. This was a look of adoration which he hadn't yet received from Julie. He now knew he had to somehow influence Victoria to discourage Julie from getting to know Flint better.

17

The rest of week progressed nicely, and everyone remained on their best behavior. Ryan, Marco, and Eric spent much of their time together with projects on which they all collaborated. Flint and Mike kept busy cleaning flower beds, watering, and giving Victoria assistance when she requested. Jasper made himself scarce and mostly took care of Ethan's errands, along with finding small projects for the crew to do.

For the remainder of the afternoon, Flint helped Victoria in the English Garden. They kept busy removing some of the old dried-out plantings and replacing them with fresh ones.

Victoria asked Flint where he was from, about his heritage, and what he planned to do with his life. The afternoon dragged, and he was occasionally ribbed by the other guys when they passed by on the tractor. Unknowing to Victoria, Marco would make sexual body motions while pointing and laughing at them. Flint found this funny, but a bit humiliating. Nevertheless, he remained a gentleman in her presence, and after a few hours it was finally time to go home.

Julie had arrived back from the train station and walked up the hill to the greenhouse. She spotted Victoria and Flint in the English Garden. Before Julie spoke, Victoria noticed Flint and Julie lock eyes.

Flint put his shovel down and greeted her. "Hi Julie. How's it going?"

Victoria stood up and looked over her shoulder. "Oh, hello dear. Flint and I have given this garden a real good cleaning. Such an improvement – don't you think?"

Julie looked back at the garden. "You've both done a superb job; it looks so much better."

Victoria looked at her watch. "Oh look, it's past five o'clock. Flint you have been a great help, and I shan't keep you another minute more. Thank you so much for your assistance."

Flint gathered all the tools and put them away in the greenhouse. He came back out, and asked Julie if she wanted to check out his new car. They separated from Victoria and walked over to the parking lot.

While Julie and Flint were checking out his car, Jasper had arrived and approached Victoria. He tipped his hat to her. "Well, doesn't this garden bed look a hundred percent better. You've really got an eye on how to improve things."

Victoria smiled, and nodded her head. "Thanks to Flint's help we managed to get so much done. He really is a hardworking young man and very polite too."

Jasper replied, "Yeah, he's good. Unlike some of the other guys, he always does what he's told. I just don't know what kind of future he has wanting to be a musician. He told me he quit school to become the next great guitar guru or something like that. I don't know. That's his business; guess he'll have to find out the hard way."

As Victoria glanced over to Julie and Flint, her expression changed to a more serious one. After a moment of contemplation, she replied to Jasper, "Well, he's young, and when you're that age, you think you know everything. I think he has promise working with plants, maybe even become a botanist or something, although that takes money. And from what I gathered, neither of his parents have very much."

Jasper shook his head in agreement, and then he changed the subject. "Say, remember I told you about the movie theater downtown? Have you given it anymore thought? Listen, why don't you talk it over with Eric and Julie and let me know. The fact of the matter is I'm not going anywhere."

Jasper politely excused himself and walked down the driveway. He looked up at Julie and Flint. Jealously erupted inside him, but he felt those remarks about Flint to Victoria would plant some seeds of doubt in her mind.

Flint reminded Julie about going hiking. "Do you still want to take a ride on Sunday to hike the *Lemon Squeeze*?"

Julie was indeed excited to explore another area, as well as have a chance to get to know Flint better. She replied, "That would be great. This place sounds awesome."

Flint smiled from ear to ear. "Alright, I'll pick you up around ten o'clock in the morning. How does that sound?"

Julie quickly looked back at her grandmother, and then back to Flint. "Perfect! I'll see you then. Thanks Flint, and good night."

Flint climbed into his primer-gray Chevy and rolled down the driveway. At that moment, he felt things were looking up. A new car and a real date with a pretty girl. Life is good, he thought to himself.

Julie returned to her grandmother, and they both silently faced the vegetable garden. Victoria looked over at Julie and noticed she was still wearing a grin on her face. She knew just what that look was all about.

Victoria asked, "Are you a little sweet on Flint? Listen dear, before you answer – let me just say something. Julie, he's a genuinely nice young man, but I feel he may be a little below your station. I mean, he comes from a low-income family and has designs on a future that is a bit unrealistic. You should try to find a young man that has a more promising future. Perhaps someone who comes from a distinguished family like your own."

Julie's fantasy was quickly halted. She was slightly angered by this remark but made effort not to show it. She loved her grandmother but didn't think she was such a snob.

Julie replied, "I get what you're saying, but what about you and Eric? He didn't go to college, and he ended up becoming a successful plumber, even starting his own business."

Victoria tilted her head and looked straight ahead. "You have me there, my dear. But with that said, life wasn't always easy for him. If it weren't for my family's money, things would have been much more difficult. Please understand, I'm not telling you what to do with your life, but I feel it's my part to give you some direction – especially, since your mother isn't around to do so."

Victoria's last remark hit a chord in Julie, but this conversation wasn't going to change her mind about spending time with Flint. After all, she really wanted to get away and explore some more of the area. Julie also knew that her mother would have really liked Flint.

That evening Nadia prepared a nice roasted turkey meal for everyone. While she was busy setting the table, King and Polly were hanging in the dining room, patiently waiting for scrap time to arrive. Nadia called for everyone to come and eat. She then opened the front door, and saw that Karl was waiting in his truck. Nadia called back inside the house. "Enjoy the meal everyone. Don't worry about the dishes; I'll do them later. Have a good evening!" Nadia put her jacket on and walked out leaving a pungent cloud of perfume that filled the kitchen.

Victoria and Eric were watching television in the living room, and Julie was busy doing some homework in her bedroom. After hearing Nadia's announcement, they all convened in the dining room and took their seats.

Eric started in about the terrorists to Victoria. "Those bastards have now set a bomb off in a subway in France, killing three people, and injuring seven. Something has to be done about this!"

After hearing Eric's announcement, Victoria was aware of the solemn look on Julie's face. She stared back at Eric and motioned her eyes in Julie's direction. Eric got her silent message and changed the subject. "So, Julie, what are working on at school right now?"

Julie snapped out of her funk. "Oh, we're learning about the different fashion trends that made the biggest impact on the world and who implemented them."

Victoria took a few bites, and stated, "Look at all of this food; it's certainly more than we can all eat. Why don't I give Jasper a call and see if he wants to join us? I'll be right back."

Eric and Julie had other things on their minds and made no remark. Instead, they continued to enjoy the meal.

Five minutes later, Jasper knocked on the front door. He popped his head in the front door and called. "Hey! Y'all, in here?"

Victoria dropped her fork, and replied, "Jasper come in; we are in the dining room!"

Jasper took a seat and smiled at everyone as he stuffed his napkin in the top of his shirt. The various plates of food were passed around, and he helped himself generously. "Man, thanks for sharing this with me. Don't think I've had a meal like this since I left Oklahoma. This is so nice – tell you what. You must allow me to treat everyone to the movies tonight. I was telling Julie about the new *Indiana Jones* movie. I know it's not on the level of *Citizen Kane* but no doubt, it's some great entertainment.

So, are you all game?" Everyone was busy chewing and agreed with a nod.

After dinner, Eric pulled the station wagon in front of the house, and everybody pilled in. On the ride to the theater the conversation was light, and Jasper managed to come up with a couple of funny stories which got everybody laughing.

Jasper would have preferred to be alone with Julie, but he knew he was still scoring points on many levels, so he resigned to sharing her and made the most of evening.

18

A couple days passed, and Sunday morning arrived. It was a beautiful day, with a clear blue sky and a nice warm breeze.

Julie sprang out of bed and slipped into her favorite blue jeans and a white blouse. She grabbed a light jacket and her pocketbook and quietly walked down-stairs.

Julie left a note where she was going and put it on the kitchen table and walked out to the front porch. Now seated in the wicker couch, Julie waited for Flint's arrival.

Several hummingbirds stopped by the hanging baskets to briefly extract some of the flowers' nectar. She then heard the faint sound of a car approaching.

Flint slowly rolled the car to a stop and waved to Julie. She quickly walked over to the car and jumped in. The hour-long drive gave them plenty of time to share their likes, dislikes, and commonalities, of which there turned out to be many. There was an easy feeling that they both felt, and the electricity started to churn between them.

A little more than an hour had passed, and the Chevy pulled into the parking lot of the *Mohonk Mountain House.*

The house was built in the early 1920's and was originally a health resort before it was later expanded into a hotel. The property had a large lake, a beautiful formal garden, and many great hiking trails. Each trail had natural, wooden gazebos located every quarter mile along the trails. These gazebos ranged in different sizes, and each offered a picturesque view of the property.

As day-hikers, they weren't supposed to enter the hotel, but they did so anyway. They grabbed a cup of tea and some of the cookies that were being served in the main lodge. Now that they were fueled, Flint and Julie walked over to the trail entrance and began their accent.

The beginning of the trail was easy to navigate. The path was fairly level, but further along it became more challenging. As such, you would have to almost get on your hands and knees to crawl underneath some of the boulders. The tight spaces put the two in proximity to one another. In one particularly tricky spot, Flint reached out his hand to help Julie back on the trail. As he pulled her up, he brought her closer to his body, and stared into her eyes. Julie reciprocated, and the two embraced and kissed.

The trail became steeper and trickier, but they both met the challenge. At each difficult point in the trail, they embraced and kissed again to celebrate their victory.

Eventually they reached the base of the *Lemon Squeeze.* This part of the path had wooden ladders that lead up a very narrow crevasse to an opening at the top. They navigated up the ladders and reached the top. As they emerged from the crevasse, they reached a clearing that had a wonderful view of the *Hudson River Valley* and the mountain ranges beyond. Both shared the feeling of victory, having accomplished this  rugged trail, and they embraced once more. At that moment, neither Flint nor Julie thought about work, school, family or being rich or poor. All they knew was it felt genuinely nice to be together.

On their way back to the Mountain House, Julie and Flint found a cozy gazebo that was close to the edge of the lake. They sat down and started talking about everybody that worked on the estate.

Flint expressed his fondness for Mike and how he was like a friendly uncle to him.

Julie replied, "I haven't had too many interactions with him, but he is sweet."

Flint indicated. "Now, Ryan and Marco. Those guys are great, but I'm really nothing like either of them, I mean..."

Julie interrupted, "You don't have to explain. I know what you mean. Good thing there are laws and rules of proper conduct, otherwise Nadia and I would have a problem with Marco."

They both laughed and then brought up the subject of Jasper. Julie asked Flint, "So, what's your take on him?"

Knowing what he did about Jasper, Flint had to ponder how he would answer her question. "I think he's definitely a strange bird, and really doesn't know how to work well with other people. I mean, the other guys are always butting heads with him. Marco manages to put him in his place, but I know underneath that Jasper's blood is boiling. Then Mike steps in and keeps things from escalating."

Julie nodded, "He is strange, but he be can very funny at times too. I think he's kind of sweet on me, but I'm in no way interested in him. I mean, obviously you get that, right?"

Flint smiled and gave Julie's hand a squeeze. "Yeah, and I'm glad to hear that. Just be careful around that guy."

Julie was somewhat perplexed by Flint's response. "Why? What do you mean by that?"

Once again, Flint had to be careful how to answer that question. He replied, "I don't know. He's from another state, and nobody really knows very much about him. He could turn out to be some serial killer or something."

Julie laughed, "Oh stop! You're too much. Alright. You don't have to convince me that he's weird."

Flint was relieved, but still neither he nor Martin knew what Jasper's true intentions were.

A few minutes passed, and Julie expressed the need to use the bathroom. "Flint, I'm going to walk over to the hotel." She gave him another kiss and left the gazebo.

Flint sat, feeling bedazzled about how the day had progressed. There didn't seem to be anyone else in the immediate area, and he was aware how everything suddenly became incredibly quiet.

Suddenly, from the side of the gazebo, a splashing sound came from the edge of the lake. Flint turned to see Martin's head looking back at him.

Martin immediately engaged with Flint. "My dear boy, I'm so glad I found you! I'm afraid that I have some rather urgent news."

Flint replied, "How did you get here, and how did you know Julie and I were here?"

Martin explained. "Remember, I told you, anywhere there is water on earth; I can connect with it. As far as knowing you two were here is another ability, but I haven't the time to explain. There have been some recent troubles in France, and this has caused indefinite delays in all flights leaving Europe. I am concerned about Ethan's safety, but also for Julie. There is no doubt she will be upset when she hears this news."

Martin continued with urgency in his voice. "Now Flint, my lad. You must return Julie soon as possible. It would be best that she be with her family when she hears of this. I plan to stay at the estate for a short time. I shall meet you back there. Now hurry and leave now my boy." With that said, Martin slid back into the water.

Flint grabbed his backpack and started walking to the Hotel to find Julie. He spotted that she was already on her way back to the lake, and he approached her. "Julie. I just noticed the time. We really should get going, and it's still another hour ride back." Julie agreed, and they made their way back to parking lot.

A little while later, Flint and Julie arrived back at the estate and approached the main house. Eric and Victoria were sitting on the front porch with concerned looks on their faces.

Flint felt a bit nervous about confronting them, so he announced to Julie, "I had a great time, and it was really nice to get to know you better, but I think it would best if I just get going."

Julie looked at him and then back at her grandparents on the porch. "Yes, perhaps so. Bye Flint, and thanks so much for today."

Julie and Flint wanted to kiss again but knew it wouldn't be a good idea in front of the grandparents.

Julie jumped out of the car, and to break the tension, she approached them with a smile. Both Victoria and Eric returned her smile, and they were relieved that she was back safe and sound.

Victoria was the first to speak, "Julie, I hope you had a good time. Thanks for leaving us the note, but I wish you would have told us about this plan before-hand."

Julie felt a little put back by her request. After all, she was an adult, and didn't feel it was necessary to ask for her permission. Nevertheless, she politely replied, "Yes, I know. Flint and I discussed this last week, but he wasn't sure if he'd make it. He showed up; so, we went. We drove to this real beautiful hotel up north and took a real cool hike on the grounds."

One of Eric's eyebrows raised when heard the mention of a hotel and responded with a pleasant smile once he understood they just went for a hike. Victoria had more reservations about this outing but decided to refrain from sharing her feelings. It was evident to her that a bit more than just conversation was exchanged.

Victoria causally stated, "Well, that's nice you two had a good time and that you were able to explore the area a little more. By the way, Jasper was wondering where you had gone. He had a question to ask you. I told him where you went, but I didn't know when you would return. He, too, was a little surprised you didn't mention anything to him about leaving today. Since your father left him in charge, he feels responsible and would have liked to have been informed."

Julie's eyes rolled, and felt a bit enraged that Jasper, of all people, was someone she would have to answer to. Once again, she bit her tongue and excused herself.

She quickly walked up to her bedroom. Polly was stretched across her bed, and Julie decided to snuggle beside her. Exhausted from the hike, she looked out the window, thought of Flint, and reflected on the day's events.

Later that evening, Julie, Victoria, and Eric were seated in the living room watching television. There was a comedy program playing and it was interrupted by a special report.

The announcer proceeded to recap the events of the bombing in France. *"Due to the recent incident in France, all travel leaving from England, France, Italy and Spain has been indefinitely suspended. Stay tuned for further developments. We will keep you updated on this situation as we learn more."*

Eric walked over to the television and turned it off. There was a look of panic on Julie's and Victoria's faces as they embraced each other.

Eric raised his hands, and calmly spoke. "Now, now, Ethan is safe at Ian's house, and this whole mess will get taken care of. There is no sense in getting all upset. We'll just have to wait a little longer to Ethan – that's all. I'll telephone him tomorrow, and you can talk to him then, Julie. I'm sure you'll feel better when you hear his voice."

After hearing the steady voice of her grandfather, Julie calmed down. Everybody gave each other a hug and went to bed. To be closer to Julie and the television, Eric and Victoria decided to stay in Ethan's room for the night.

Julie lay awake in bed for a while before falling asleep. She couldn't stop thinking about her father. After a couple of deep breaths, she started to wind down. She heard a car door close outside the house, and new it must be Nadia returning from her evening with Karl. Julie was comforted by her return, and soon feel asleep after a very exhausting and emotional day.

19

The next morning, Mike rolled into the parking lot and popped out of his car, he stood in front of the garden fence, and reached for one of his smokes. He lit the match, inhaled, and released a slow stream of smoke in the air.

The stillness of the morning was interrupted by the sound of rock music approaching the greenhouse. Ryan and Marco, who usually car-pooled together, flew into the parking lot.

Flint immediately followed, and parked next to Ryan. He jumped out of his car, wearing a big smile on his face.

Ryan was the first to notice the change in Flint's disposition. "I take it you and Julie got together yesterday?"

Marco quickly interjected, "So, did you sweat her? You know, go all the way? I want details my man – fill me in."

Flint bashfully replied, "No. But we kissed quite a bit, and I think we might have something going on."

Mike overheard Marco's questionnaire and smiled while shaking his head. Everybody then huddled in front of the garden next to Mike. The topic of the terrorist activity was brought up again, and Ryan mentioned he heard that the United States might even activate a mandatory draft.

Marco boasted, "I'll go! Just let me at those sons-of-bitches. I'll take their water-pipe and shove it up their ass. Then I'll put a bullet in their head." He then followed that remark with a cackling laugh.

Flint couldn't bear the thought of going to war. He had just met his dream girl, and certainly had no desire to be soldier. As a musician and a nature lover, Flint just couldn't conceive the killing of another human being.

All the chatter came to an abrupt halt when Jasper's truck pulled into the parking lot followed by Eric and King in the golf cart.

Everybody exchanged good mornings, and Eric made the announcement that Ethan's return was detained due to flight restrictions leaving Europe. Eric elaborated. "I spoke to him, and he wants everybody to stay calm and keep busy."

Eric then turned to Jasper, "I'm going to need Ryan and Marco with me today. The pipes in the bathroom and kitchen at the cabin need to be replaced. It's a big job, and I'll need them both – if that's alright with you?"

Both Ryan and Marco gave Eric an assertive nod.

Jasper had other plans for them on this day, but he stepped back, raised his hands and said, "Alright. You guys do what you got to do. Flint, I need you to clean out the chicken coup, and muck the goat's stall. It hasn't been done in a while, so I appreciate if you would get on it."

Jasper made it a point to come up with a nasty job for Flint. He wanted to make him suffer for taking Julie out behind his back.

He continued. "Mike, I think Victoria has some things for you to water, so just give her a hand. Thank you." The group disbanded, and everyone went about their business.

Jasper needed to give some thought about Ethan's delay. He knew that once Ethan returned, his free reign would end. He was already finding it difficult to circumvent Eric and Victoria.

With all this metal energy being spent, Jasper decided

he needed to rejuvenate himself. He walked down to the pond, morphed into his frog form, and entered the water. Jasper then opened his eyes and was startled by the presence of Martin floating right in front of him. He was taken back and assumed an aggressive position. With a negative tone, he asked, "What are you doing here?"

Martin replied, "Well, it's nice to see you too, ole' chap. What, pray tell, have you been up to since I've been gone?"

In a smug manner, Jasper replied, "That's my business, and if you haven't noticed, everything is simply fine without you around. What are you doing back? I thought you were with your dear Ethan?"

Martin was getting angry, and weary of Jasper's rudeness. "Look here, frog's breath, I want to know what your interest is with Julie and how much longer you plan to stick around?"

Jasper coldly replied, "Julie will belong to me soon, and there's nothing you, Ethan or Flint can do about it. He then pointed at the round rock at the bottom of the bridge. Like I stated to you before, my time is almost done here, and once I go through that opening with Julie, it will be sealed forever!"

Shocked by this information, Martin advanced closer to Jasper. "My good man, you can't possibly think you have the right to remove Julie from her family and life here? Don't you have any concern for her? Furthermore, do you really think she will be resigned to a life happily-ever-after with you in your foreign dimension!"

Jasper replied, "I can be everything she needs; she just doesn't realize this yet. My powers will be enhanced once I return to my own environment, so you better stay out of my way. Don't forget, I can leave the water, and you cannot. So just be a good little serpent and stay on your side of the pond."

Martin couldn't believe what he was hearing and was dumbfounded how this creature could be so cold.

Now filled with rage, Martin responded, "Mr. Jasper, your time here is no doubt going to come to an end, and I will make sure of this. You have no idea of my powers either!" Martin quickly recoiled, and rapidly swan to the other of the pond.

Little did Jasper know the network of assistance Martin had assembled. Martin's priority was to gather his allies and inform them on what Jasper planned to do. Concerned about Julie, Martin was beside himself.

Currently all the workers were busy on different parts of the estate. If there was anybody he could possibly contact, it would be the fairies.

Foster and Faye were highly in-tune to their surroundings and might be receptive to Martin's thought waves. He closed his eyes and began sending them a message.

Foster was busy in the English Garden harvesting some milk of the poppy. While doing so, he helped himself to a few drops. Since he was mildly pickled, this prevented him from receiving any messages that Martin was trying to send.

Faye was inside the greenhouse admiring the bird of paradise plant. She quickly picked up Martin's message and was keenly aware of a voice in her head. She stood away from the plant and made more effort to tap into this contact.

After a few moments, the message came into her consciousness, and she recognized the British accent. It was noticeably clear to her that Martin was repeating, "Fairies – come to the pond – now!"

Faye jumped to the floor and ran outside to get Foster. She approached him and was miffed to find him in a slight stupor.

Foster turned to her with a big smile on his face, and said, "What's cooking, Woobie bear?"

Faye grabbed his hand, and said, "In the middle of the day, dear? You're as bad as Marco. Get you head together.

Martin has just summoned us to the pond!"

Foster's eyes got wider. "Really? I though he was with Ethan in England?"

"So did I." said Faye. "Hurry now! Put that stuff away, and let's go!"

Hand in hand, they sprinted down through the trees and came out of the woods by the playhouse. At that moment, Emily was peering out the front door window and spotted them. She passed through the silo wall to head them off.

Faye and Foster then stopped in their tracks. Faye addressed her. "Hello Emily. I'm afraid we haven't come to pay a social visit. Rather, we are on an important mission to see someone down at the pond. You must excuse us."

"Really? Who are you meeting there?" asked Emily.

Foster nervously replied, "Ah, you don't know this person."

Emily replied, "Oh. You mean the serpent. I've seen him. He's exceptionally beautiful, but I never introduced myself. Do you mind if I come along?"

Faye looked at Foster and then back up at Emily. "Well, why not. Let's not waste any more time."

The Fairies and Emily soon arrived at the south end of the pond and waited underneath a small maple tree. A few moments passed, and Martin's large head slowly emerged from the water. He looked back at the stone bridge to make sure Jasper wasn't anywhere near and smiled down at them. "You received my message, and I see you've brought a friend too. This is particularly good because we will need all the help we can muster."

Foster gestured, "This is Emily. She lives... or used to live here. She wants to help."

Martin replied, "Pleased to make your acquaintance

young lady."

Martin looked back at the fairies, and immediately filled them in. "I've just had a very disturbing conversation with that bloody creature, Jasper. He explained to me that his time is nearly ended here. This is fine by me, but he also plans to capture Julie and bring her back with him."

The fairies looked at each other in horror. Faye spoke quietly, "We thought you were in England with Ethan, so what are you doing back?"

Martin shook his head side to side. "Apparently, flights have been detained and Ethan is unable to return right now. We must form a plan of action against Jasper until Ethan returns. First, you must let Mike and Flint know of Jasper's full intentions. Meanwhile, I will investigate Jasper's portal and see if there's any way I can access my way in. I don't think he can fully return before his time, so let me see what I can do."

Martin momentarily looked at Emily. "Since you are able to move about unseen, you could be very useful."

Emily replied, "Well, everybody except Jasper. I mean, if he concentrates hard enough, I do become visible to him. It seems he becomes weak if he's been away from water for too long."

"I see," replied Martin. "Well, do what you can and when I've come up with a plan – we shall all meet again. Thank you very much. I'm counting on each one of you." As quick as Martin appeared, he swiftly submerged back into the water.

Flint was still busy cleaning the chicken coup. He had a pinched look on his face due to the horrible stench of the feces. He cursed Jasper for making him do this chore, but he kept his mind occupied by thinking of Julie's sweet kisses. Also, the thought of possibly going to war was weighing heavy on him. He hoped the military would accept enough volunteers before having to issue the draft.

Mike had finished helping Victoria water the flower baskets in the bath house and was coming to check in on Flint. The chicken coup was connected to the barn opposite the vegetable garden.

Mike decided to cut across the garden on his way to the barn. He was about half-way across, when he saw a daisy moving from side to side on top one of the fence posts.

As Mike approached the moving flower, he saw that Foster and Faye were standing there wearing serious looks on their faces. Mike got closer and asked, "Oh no. What's going on?"

Faye told Mike about the horror Jasper had in mind for Julie. She then explained to him all about Martin.

After hearing this, Mike was once again stunned. He thought – fairies, a creature from another dimension, and now a serpent! What's next?

Now aware of Jasper's full intentions, Mike's first reaction was to contact the authorities. However, he quickly dismissed this idea. After all, telling the police his employers' daughter was about to be abducted by a shape-shifting creature from another dimension just wouldn't fly.

Foster explained further. "Listen, Martin, the serpent is trying to find a way to send this creature back, so we can be rid of him for once and all. However, Martin can't leave the water and he needs our assistance so we think you should inform Flint about what's going on!"

Faye could see that Mike was becoming flustered. "Martin has been with Mr. Clark and his family since he was boy. He can only travel in water, but he has the capability to read people and communicate telepathically. Flint knows of Martin, but he's been instructed not to tell anyone."

In frustration, Mike raised his head skyward, and winced his eyes. He took a deep breath and looked back down at the fairies. Upon re-opening his eyes, he stepped back in bewilderment by the visible presence of Emily. He instantly recognized her from when she lived on the estate. Once again, Mike questioned his sanity, and muttered, "This just gets weirder by the minute – Jiminy Crickets, lucky me."

Emily looked up at Mike, "Thank you for keeping this place looking so nice. You were always exceedingly kind to me. I can move about the estate without being seen and want to help in any way I can."

Mike gave up trying to figure out what was happening to him and resigned himself to the situation at hand. "Look, I'll talk to Flint. Furthermore, I think it's time I met this serpent too. So, count me in on your next meeting."

All nodded and separated. Mike then started walking in the direction of the barn.

Once again, Mike thought to himself, "I'm getting too old for this kind stuff." To clear his head, he leaned against the barn and decided to contemplate this situation with a smoke. He immediately felt that Ryan, Marco, Nadia, Eric, and Victoria should be left out of this. However, for the sake of her own safety, he believed Julie should be included. No doubt she should be made aware of what Jasper really planned to do with her. Mike finished his smoke and walked over to the chicken coop to inform Flint.

Once he arrived, Mike sat Flint down and explained to Flint about Jasper's plans for Julie. He also filled him in about Foster, Faye, and little Emily.

Flint was both enraged and frightened after hearing this.

Mike could see he was getting flustered. "Alright kid – just calm down. We are all planning to meet with the serpent to come up with a plan. Timing is the most important thing, and we can't let Jasper know we're onto him.

Now, I also think it's important to let Julie know what's going on too. But only her, and no one else, especially crazy Marco. God only knows what he would do."

Flint was now able to relax and gained control of himself. "You're right Mike. Jesus, this whole thing is so insane. I mean, what the hell are we mixed up in? Up until now, I thought things like sea serpents, fairies and inter-dimensional beings were just pure fantasy."

Mike shook his head in agreement. "Me too kid. Nevertheless, this situation is very real, and we need to do our part, whatever that ends up being. After I talk to the fairies, I'll let you know when we plan to meet. Just keep your cool kid. And remember – dummy up."

20

The following week arrived, and since the plumbing in the cabin had to be renovated, Victoria and Eric had permanently moved into the main house.

That morning Nadia entered the house after dropping Julie off at the train station. She quickly entered the kitchen and almost bumped into Victoria who was preparing breakfast for herself and Eric.

Slightly surprised, Nadia said, "Oh, I was going to fix you breakfast; you don't have to do that."

Victoria replied, "Nonsense, my dear. I really do enjoy cooking, and Eric and I have been up for a while. Unfortunately, we've been stressing about this terrorist activity."

Nadia hung her coat and sat down at the breakfast table. "You must try to relax about this situation."

Eric had his face buried in the morning paper, and then dropped it on the table. "Says here that the United States and France are planning to deploy troupes in the middle east. Looks like there's a much bigger threat behind all of this. Also, they are encouraging young men and women to join the military. I'm afraid we might lose some of our crew as well. I heard Ryan and Marco talking about joining the air force, and, in their words, they wanted to blow those fuckers to kingdom come. I support them. Nice to see there are still some fighting men left in the world."

Victoria and Nadia looked at each other with solemn looks on their faces. Eric was aware of this and realized he better dial things down a notch. He lightly spoke, "Ethan's going to be fine. I also saw that most of the airlines plan to reinstate service in a couple days so before you know it, he'll be back here with us."

King and Polly were also in the kitchen. King was half-parked under the kitchen table, and Polly was sitting by the window, soaking up the morning sunlight. After finishing their breakfast, the three humans left the kitchen.

King stood up and moved next to Polly. "I don't have a good feeling about Ethan, and I'm worried for him."

Polly looked out the window, and back at King. "You heard Eric; he'll be back in a couple days. There's no need to get your biscuits in a bind, big guy."

King cocked his head. "You cats! It's so easy for you to have such a laissez faire attitude about everything. I miss him and feel that something bad could happen."

"Nonsense!" hissed Polly. "He will return, and I'm sure of it. Now get yourself together and stop breathing on me. Go lay back down."

Polly felt unsure as well but didn't want to voice it in front of King. She felt it was better not to worry about things until they happened. Polly then returned to looking out the window.

By this time, Jasper had returned from his morning errands. He parked his truck at the greenhouse and waited for the crew to arrive.

The crew pulled into to the parking lot, got out of their cars and stretched. Jasper climbed out of his truck, carrying a bag of chainsaw blades and bar oil. He then approached the crew. "Say guys, I've got a project for y'all to do. The stone wall between us and the golf course needs to be cleared. If I can have everybody on this program, we can knock it off in one day. How about it?"

Looks darted between Ryan and Marco. Then Marco stepped forward. "Listen. Me and Ryan are working with Eric, and right now we're right in the middle of big job."

Jasper slowly shook his head up and down. "Yeah, I know that, and I've already got permission from Eric to have you guys for this program."

Marco glared back at Jasper. He turned and spit on the ground and then walked back next to Ryan.

Jasper extended the bag to Mike. "Here ya' go; got y'all some new blades. Should make the job go quicker. You guys have a good time. I'll check back with ya' later." Jasper confidently climbed back in his truck and took off down the hill.

Mike and Flint went inside the greenhouse to gather some tools for the job. Ryan and Marco started walking towards the barn to fetch the tractor and cursed Jasper for pulling them away from Eric.

While Mike and Flint were inside the greenhouse, Faye and Foster jumped down on the shelf and got Mike's attention. Mike stopped what he was doing, tapped Flint on the shoulder, and pointed to the top shelf.

To Flint's amazement, the fairies peered back at him. Faye smiled at him and spoke first. "Pleased to finally meet you, Flint. This is my mate Foster. We've been watching and listening to you since we arrived. I'm happy that you and Julie have become better acquainted."

Foster was eager to let them know about the meeting with Martin. "Hello Flint. I'm sure Mike has told you about our meeting with Martin. He wants us all to meet him at the pond today. Are you guys up for this?"

Mike and Flint both looked at each other, and then Mike replied, "Yes, we'll be there."

Faye replied, "Good. Then its settled. We'll see you both later."

The snapping sound of the tractor motor approached the greenhouse and the fairies darted back up into the loft. Mike and Flint brought the tools out to the trailer and jumped on.

The morning progressed, and for most of the day the chainsaws echoed throughout the estate. Presently, everybody was at different ends of the property. Even Nadia and Victoria had left for another visit to the nursery.

Lunchtime had passed, and Jasper decided to check on the progress of the crew. He arrived at the stone wall and saw that everybody was busy stacking the cut branches in a large pile. The wall was now cleared, and it made Jasper happy that he got the guys to follow his orders. He drove his truck slowly across the grass field and parked next to the brush pile.

Jasper rolled down his window and called over to the crew. "Real good job – I'm proud of you guys. The boss will be happy this job was completed. Listen, I'll load some of this brush into the back of my truck and dump it in the woods. Flint, why don't you give me a hand."

Flint walked over next to Jasper, and the two started loading the truck. Jasper asked, "So, how's that new car treating you? Must be nice to have your own wheels. Say, where did you and Julie go last weekend?"

Flint knew where this was going and decided to play along. "We took a ride to a real nice mountain lodge up north, and then hiked a few trials. We had a good time. She really enjoyed seeing a different area besides this one."

Jasper nodded his head. "Well, that sounds good, but I wouldn't get your hopes up about dating her. I've already spoken to Victoria, and she'd rather have Julie involved with someone who... how should I put this, has more direction in life. You know what I mean, something more than just being a musician."

Flint didn't care to discuss this subject with Jasper. So, he confidently replied, "Jasper, we're just two young people hanging out, and having a good time."

Jasper didn't get the reaction he was hoping for. Instead, he replied, "I here ya'. After all, there's plenty of hens in the chicken coup. Right?"

Once again, Flint knew Jasper was trying to derail any hopes of continuing a relationship with Julie. Nevertheless, Flint reminded himself that Martin's plan would hopefully put an end to this disturbing creature once and for all.

They finished filling the truck with branches, and Jasper announced that he would unload the truck himself.

After Jasper left, Marco approached Flint. "What was that shit-for-brains talking to you about?"

Flint chuckled, "He told me Victoria thinks I'm a loser, and I better forget about any chances with Julie."

Marco looked up at Flint. "Fuck that guy, and fuck Queen Victoria too! Just screw her and move on. No doubt, you'll have a challenge trying to fit in with that family. Who knows? You might be flying over to the middle east soon."

Flint wasn't inspired by Marco's point of view, or the thought of fighting in any war. He simply replied, "Well as far as both those things go, I'm not going to do anything that doesn't feel right."

Marco didn't grasp Flint's logic and walked back over by Ryan. The two launched into a debate about which beer they liked the most.

Mike quickly grew bored with their conversation and

walked over next to Flint. He looked at his watch and whispered, "Hey kid. I bet Julie is going to be home in a couple minutes. Why do you take a walk over to the main house and tell her about our meeting later?"

Flint nodded his head. "Sounds good Mike. I'll tell these guys I need a sit-down bathroom break." Flint yelled over to the other guys, and they briefly shook their heads.

Flint made his way across the field and cut past the bath house on his way to the main house. Upon arriving, he saw that Nadia, Victoria and Julie had just pulled into the driveway.

Nadia and Julie both saw Flint and gave him a big smile. However, Victoria just stared ahead, wearing a neutral look on her face.

Julie got out of the car, and approached Flint, "Hey, good to see you. How did your day go? Hope it was better than mine. I've been just burdened with more homework."

Flint wanted to give her a kiss, but with Victoria in their presence, he knew it wouldn't be a good idea. Instead, he played it cool and gave Julie a brief explanation of his day.

Nadia and Victoria walked into the house, while Julie remained behind. "Flint, I really need to get busy working on a couple projects, but it's good to see you. Maybe we can get together again this coming weekend or something. Let's chat on Friday and see how the week plays out. Does that sound alright with you?"

Flint nodded, and then looked about to see if anyone was nearby. "Julie, could I ask a favor of you? A little after five o'clock, Mike and I are planning to meet at the little gazebo down by the pond. We have something important to tell you about Jasper. So, its real important that you be there. I can't tell you what it's all about right now, but it will only take a few minutes. Alight?"

Julie was somewhat confused by this request but figured it would give her a chance to see Flint afterwards. "Sure Flint, no problem. I'll see you later. Bye now."

Flint stood smiling in the driveway with his head in the clouds. He then noticed the outline of Emily coming into focus on the wicker couch.

Sitting there, she smiled, gave him two thumbs up, and vanished. Flint collected himself, turned around and headed back to report with Mike.

Since Jasper was busy unloading brush in the woods, Martin decided to swim over and investigate his layer. Martin surfaced by the stone bridge and dove down to the base of the bridge where the portal was located. Martin wanted to see if he could possibly enter his dimension, so he floated in front of the circular rock for several minutes.

After a few attempts, he successfully penetrated through to the other side. Martin surveyed the surroundings and deduced that the inhabitants of this dimension must be advanced. He also hoped they weren't all like Jasper. Fearing he may not be able to return, Martin quickly returned to the pond. He was able to do so and now felt confident he could save Julie. He then left quickly and was now prepared to discuss his plan with the others.

A little while later, Jasper returned from emptying the truck and pulled into the parking lot by the greenhouse. Foster and Faye were on their way to meet with Martin and remained frozen to see which direction Jasper would go. After seeing that he remained sitting in his truck, they darted into the woods.

Just after they crossed the road, the clapping sound of the tractor flew past the greenhouse, and it stopped next to Jasper's truck. Ryan shut off the tractor and everyone jumped out.

Mike lit one of his cigarettes, and Marco extracted a hand-rolled one from his shirt pocket. Jasper made a face, but knew it was futile arguing with Marco. After all, in a couple weeks he would be done with this place and the crew.

Mike didn't really get the whole getting high thing, but as far as he could see, it didn't affect the guy's work ability. Instead, it seems to keep them happy and focused with only one exception – it made Marco way too chatty.

The topic of joining the service was brought up again. It was at this time that Marco made the announcement that he and Ryan planned to join the air force. They were going to wait until Ethan returned to give their notice, but given the circumstances, they decided not to delay it any longer.

Flint was aware of their plans but remained detached for fear of being ridiculed for not wanting to join as well.

Jasper asked Flint, "What about you? Are you going too?"

Mike interrupted. "The kid ain't going if he doesn't have to. Not if I can help it. Primarily because I need him here to help me with the fall cleanup. I can't take care of everything. Understand?"

Jasper listened to Mike's statement and looked back to Flint. "Guess you're in the clear – unless they draft your ass."

Marco interjected, "Yeah Mike, they might even draft your ass over there!" Everyone laughed, and the topic was dropped.

The end of the workday had finally arrived. Marco and Ryan exited the estate with their music blasting from the open car windows and Jasper left to take a ride into town. Mike and Flint were now in route to meet with

Martin and the others.

After hearing Ryan's car go by, Julie stopped what she was working on and quietly walked downstairs. She slipped out the back door and made her way to the gazebo.

Mike and Flint were already sitting near the gazebo. Julie walked over and sat beside them. Flint reached his arm around her back and planted a quick kiss. Mike smiled at her and exhaled the last drag of his cigarette.

Julie opened by saying, "I have some exciting news! Father called today and said he may be able to return very soon. Isn't that great!"

Mike shook his head. "Now, that is good news. I've definitely got a few things to discuss with him when he returns."

Julie looked at them both. "So... what's going on? Flint said, you guys had something to tell me about Jasper. Other than he's only plain strange."

Mike looked Julie straight in the eyes. "What you probably already know is that Jasper fancies you, but there is more than meets the eye with this guy. Flint and I have known this for a while now, and because of some recent information we've been given, we feel it's time to let you in a few things."

Julie looked back and forth at Mike and Flint. "What? Is he wanted by the police or something?"

Flint reached over and touched Julie on the shoulder. "What we are about to explain to you is going to blow your mind, but I assure you it's all very real.

Flint slowly explained the whole story behind Jasper, Martin and the other creatures living on the estate. After he finished, Julie sat with a look of astonishment and disbelief on her face.

Mike could tell that she must be thinking the two of them made this whole story up. So, he explained further. "Julie, we aren't crazy, and in few minutes, you will have proof of what Flint has just explained to you. The fairies, Emily, and the serpent, want to reveal themselves to you as well. This way we can all come up with a plan to get rid of Jasper."

Julie still didn't fully comprehend the whole story, and replied, "So my dad has had a serpent from another star system watching over him, and there's also been two fairies flying around! Plus, this place has a ghost of a little girl who once lived here. Guys, I do have a broad imagination. As a matter of fact, my mother believed in fairies and always wanted to see one. However, I'm having a real hard time grasping all of this and..."

Just at that moment, Julie was quickly silenced by a loud splash and the sound of dripping water. A green light was then cast on all three of them, and Julie turned her head toward the pond.

Staring back at her was Martin. He was perched halfway out of the water, wearing a huge grin.

Julie couldn't believe what she was seeing and felt she was about to have a panic attack. Martin could sense her reaction and knew she needed help. Just like he had done with Flint, Martin calmed her down. This was also Mike's first meeting with Martin. He thought to himself, "Alright, I've seen everything now."

Martin calmly spoke. "Dear Julie, I don't mean to frighten you. I never expected this meeting would ever have to take place. You must understand it's especially important that you are made aware of the circumstances that lay before you. This man called Jasper is not what he appears to be. He is from another dimension that has been observing this earth. You might say he is a criminal that has been sentenced here. His time is almost ended, but before returning he wants you to join him. We want to make sure this doesn't take place."

With a look of horror on her face, Julie looked back at Flint and Mike. "How long have you known about this?"

Mike was about to reply, when his eyes were drawn to the ground at the edge of the pond. Julie turned her head in the direction Mike was looking, and to her amazement, there stood Foster and Faye. They were hand in hand looking up at her, both wearing wide and comforting smiles.

Faye spoke first. "Julie, my name is Faye, and this is my mate Foster. We have been with your family since you were a child. Like Martin explained, we too would not be revealing ourselves to you if this wasn't important.

Faye continued. "First, we are deeply sorry for the loss of your mother. She was truly a beautiful soul. Second, we will assist you with all our power to protect you from Jasper. Finally, we have one more companion to introduce you to. Her name is Emily, and she is a spirit that resides on the estate. She is the ghost of the young child who died here years ago.

Emily suddenly appeared, standing behind Mike with her hands on his shoulders. "Hello Julie. Please don't be scared. We are all here to help you. Oh, by the way, I love your hair – long and wavy like mine."

Foster grounded the conversation, and added, "Julie. This must be very overwhelming for you, especially since your father is stuck in England right now. We know that Jasper doesn't plan to do anything to you until it's time for him to return. So, it's important that you not let on that you are aware of his identity or intentions."

The shock of witnessing this strange group of companions, was a bit overwhelming. Julie pulled herself closer to Flint and looked back at each one of them.

Martin spoke in a calm, and reassuring voice. "Julie,

as you can see, we all have our powers and strengths. I promise that nothing bad will happen to you. Now, I have inspected the portal to Jasper's dimension, and I have even visited this place. Listen carefully. I have a plan, but it can only be implemented on the day he has to return. Trust me, with all of us working together, we can defeat this dreadful misfit.

Julie was now more relaxed and felt comforted by all the support. She turned her attention to Martin. "Does my father know about Jasper, and what he plans to do?"

Martin moved closer to the bank of the pond. "I'm afraid not. Ethan doesn't know of my existence, and I am unable to leave the water. However, I can impact some important decisions on his behalf, but I'm afraid meeting him face to face is out of the question, especially, since he's now staying at Ian's house."

Flint suddenly came up with an idea, and asked Martin. "Say, would you be able to bring Julie and myself back to England with you? This way, we could tell Mr. Clark ourselves."

Julie replied, "Yes. There is a small lake on our old property, and it's only a mile from Ian's house. You could leave us there, and we could walk to Ian's house."

Everyone turned to Martin and waited for his reply. Martin cocked his head and took a moment to contemplate this request. "Well, it is possible to take the both of you, but this will have to be done soon, and without anyone else knowing. You must be here exceedingly early in the morning, so I can have you back before anyone knows you've left.

Julie and Flint excitingly looked at each other. Julie replied, "We will both meet you here at four o'clock tomorrow morning. Is that alright with you Flint?" Flint quickly shook his head in agreement.

Martin looked back to the stone bridge, and then made eye contact with everyone. "Thank you all for coming.

Going forward, we must keep a close watch on Jasper's every move. Julie and Flint, I shall meet you here in the morning." Martin then disappeared back into the water.

The fairies and Emily also left, leaving Mike, Flint and Julie standing under the willow tree. Mike lit a cigarette and took a couple long drags. "This whole thing is quite unbelievable, but I'm proud of you kid. And Julie, now that you know what's going on, try to conceal this information from your grandparents. Also, just carry on with Jasper like nothing has changed. I'll see you kids tomorrow. Oh, and enjoy the trip, and give my best to Mr. Clark. Goodnight, you two."

Flint and Julie gave each other a quick hug and a kiss, and Flint said, "I'll see you here tomorrow. Don't worry, this will all work out. I have faith in the serpent. Martin is quite fascinating, isn't he?" Julie quietly nodded but remained in a state of bewilderment.

Julie walked back up to the main house. She quietly went upstairs to her bedroom and proceeded to immerse herself in homework in order take her mind off from what had just transpired.

21

The following morning, Flint arose early and left in the dark to meet Julie and Martin. As he approached the entrance to the estate, he turned off the headlights so he wouldn't attract attention. The last person he wanted to awaken was Jasper. Flint exited onto the dirt road past the cabin and parked at the end of the road near the stone pillars. He quietly closed the door and walked to the weeping willow tree next to the pond.

The morning air was cool, and there was a light breeze that made the leaves rustle in the trees. Flint was excited to visit England but was baffled on how Martin was going pull this off.

Just then, Julie came from behind and tapped Flint on his shoulder. They both embraced, when suddenly a swoosh followed by a couple drops of water splashed onto them. Martin appeared, and whispered, "You made it, good. Hold each other's hand and remain still."

Martin lifted himself almost completely out of the water. From the center of his head a transparent green bubble grew until it surrounded both Flint and Julie.

With both now engulfed in the light, Martin lifted them off the ground, and arranged the bubble in front of his chest. He then plunged into the water and started swimming to the bottom of the pond.

Julie and Flint looked at each other in awe of what was taking place. Not only could they breathe normally, but they were able see everything before them.

Martin proceeded to swim to the bottom of the pond. Before reaching the bottom, he then projected another beam of light that bore a hole in the ground. This beam made an opening large enough for them to pass through. Within a short period of time, they spilled into the Hudson river.

The glowing light that emanated from Martin allowed Julie and Flint to make out different objects that had sunken to the bottom of the river. Various wrecked boats, cars, and rotted decking from bygone time periods could be seen. There were even a couple of skeletons tied to cinder blocks, just like Ryan described had been done to unwanted, trouble-making county workers.

Martin swam to the center of the river, and then accelerated forward at a magnificent speed. Flint and Julie could no longer see anything but the green light that surrounded them. The sound of the rushing water became louder and louder. It was at this time, Martin placed them both asleep. He continued onward through the river, and eventually into the Atlantic Ocean.

After several hours, Martin slowed down, and the two awoke to see the shore walls of England approaching. Martin created another opening in the earth, and they shortly arrived at the pond at Julie's old house. Martin maneuvered the bubble onto the bank and released them both. It was now five hours later in England, and the sun was shining. Julie was thrilled to be back at her old home again. Flint was still reveling at what had just happened and was even more happy to be back on solid ground.

Martin smiled at them both. "Here you go. I will wait

here but do hurry. You don't have very much time. Remember, we need to get you back before breakfast time in New York. Just explain to Ethan what's going on and return promptly."

Julie nodded her head, and the two started walking to Ian's house.

Currently, Ethan was sitting on Ian's front porch. He was busy writing some lesson plans, and from the corner of his eye he noticed two people approaching the house. He didn't quite recognize the young man, but the other, to his astonishment, looked just like Julie.

As the two came closer, Ethan immediately stood up, and dropped the papers from his hand. "Julie, is that you? And Flint? What on earth! How did you both get here?"

Julie didn't say anything, but instead ran and embraced her father. She stepped back and wiped the tears out of her eyes. "Dad. Flint and I have something to tell you, but you better sit down for this."

Julie explained to Ethan all about Jasper, Martin, the fairies, and Emily the ghost. She let her father know that Mike, too, had been doing all he could to assist her. In short detail, Julie described how Martin brought them both to England. Flint explained more about Jasper, and what he really was.

Ethan allowed them to finish, but he was flabbergasted by the whole story. "Alright. Jokes over you guys. You two managed to catch a flight over here, and this whole story was contrived to soften my reaction about you coming without my permission. Right?"

Flint shook his head and looked Ethan in the eye. "Honest, Mr. Clark, I know this all sounds beyond belief, but everything we've told you is true. We do need to return very soon, but you must call Jasper or something. Maybe tell him now that Eric and Victoria are living there, they can take over his responsibilities. Perhaps if he is forced to leave, he might change his mind and find some other girl to bring back with him."

Julie turned to her father. "The serpent says he has a plan, and I trust he does. Nevertheless, we all agreed that you should know what's going on too. I know we could have just called you about this. But, Dad, I was so scared and needed to see you."

Now having accepted the gravity of this situation, Ethan replied calmly, "I'm overly concerned, and hopefully I'll be able to return in a couple of days. The fact is, I could come back with you now, although too many questions would be raised about how I managed to return so soon. Julie, you know I love you and wouldn't let anything happen to you. Mike is right. Don't tell your grandparents, and we certainly can't let Jasper know we are onto him. I will call and speak to Mike about all this. In the meantime, I need to come up with something to tell Jasper. Flint, I think your idea is a good one, and I'll give it some thought. Best that you both return now. I still can't get over how you arrived here. Utterly amazing! I certainly would like to meet this serpent; he sounds remarkably interesting."

Ethan shook Flint's hand and thanked him for helping Julie. Julie wiped more tears from her face and gave her father a long embrace. Julie and Flint then left to meet with Martin.

They soon arrived back at the pond. Within seconds, Martin appeared and scooped them up in the same manner as before. Then the serpent plunged back into the pond and, without haste, began their speedy journey back to New York.

A few hours later, Martin burst from surface of the pond at Woodlands. He placed Julie and Flint back on the shore.

Exhausted from the round-trip journey, Martin whispered, "Looks like the sun is just starting to rise, so you two need to hurry back without being seen. As for myself, I need to rest from all this traveling. Get together with Mike, the fairies and Emily when you have a chance. I can communicate with Faye easily, and will do so when needed. Now run along."

Julie walked up the hill and quietly entered back into the main house using the back patio entrance. Flint returned to his car and drove back to the main driveway. He came to the end of the dirt road and turned right towards the main house.

As he approached the stone bridge, he spotted Jasper walking back to the gatehouse. Jasper was returning from his morning rejuvenation.

Flint wondered if Jasper had witnessed, he and Julie return, but as much as he didn't want to stop, he knew he had to.

Flint stopped the car and rolled down the window. "Morning Jasper. What's the program for today?"

Jasper bent closer to Flint's open car window. "You're a little early Flint. What's up? You look a little tired. What's the matter – couldn't sleep?"

Flint quickly replied, "Yeah, I had a rough night, Jasper. I also had to make a few stops before coming here."

Jasper just stood there and gave Flint a blank stare. The silence was broken when Mike pulled up right behind Flint's car. Mike threw his hands up as if to imply what's the hold-up?

Jasper stood up straight and waved back at Mike. Flint took this opportunity to advance forward to dodge any further interaction with Jasper. Mike followed Flint and simply nodded to Jasper as he passed.

Jasper continued walking back to gatehouse, and saw

that Marco and Ryan were approaching. As they passed, Marco let out big cloud of marijuana smoke in his direction. Jasper shook his head in disgust, thinking to himself – it's going to be one of those days.

On the other side of the Atlantic, Ethan was giving serious thought about how to deal with Jasper and the whole situation. He, too, considered contacting the authorities but arrived at the same conclusion as Mike. After throwing a couple ideas back and forth, he decided to wait a couple more days. After all, there seemed to be enough protection for Julie back on the estate. Ethan pondered that if he could only return to the estate, he would have a better understanding on how to handle all this. Providing the ban would be lifted, Ethan decided to call the airport and made a tentative reservation for a flight leaving that Friday.

Ethan waited a couple of hours, and then called the estate. Nadia picked up of the phone. "Hello, Clark residence. How may I help you?"

Ethan warmly replied, "Nadia dear, it's me Ethan. How are you?"

"Wonderful! When are you coming home? We all miss you very much, especially Julie!"

Ethan rapidly replied, "Listen. I've booked a flight for this coming Friday. But Nadia, I have another favor to ask. Would you mind getting Mike for me? I don't mind waiting. Thank you, and I hope to see you all very soon."

"Certainly. He and Flint are helping Victoria out front, hold on." Nadia placed the receiver on the kitchen table and walked outside. She announced to Mike that Ethan was on the phone.

Mike excused himself, walked in the main house, and picked up the receiver. "Mr. Clark? Mike here, how are things with you?"

Ethan informed Mike that he might be able return by the end of the week. Ethan immediately alerted Mike that he knew of the situation. He then explained that he planned to diplomatically deal with Jasper when he returned.

Mike agreed. "Yeah, we don't want to put out a fire with gasoline. I'm not sure what this character is capable of, but according to the serpent, Jasper is only a week away from returning to where he came from. Unfortunately, we will have to wait until that time to deal with him."

Ethan replied, "Yes Mike, so I've been told. I'm sorry we have brought you into this mess."

"Well, Mr. Clark, it certainly has been a strange ride. After becoming acquainted with all these various creatures, I'll be glad when things get back to normal here. By the way, Marco and Ryan wanted me to let you know they're planning on enlisting to fight for their country. I think they have all the right to do so if they want. Me and kid can take of the fall cleanup."

"I understand fully. Please, let them know that it's alright with me and to leave whenever they wish. Glad you and Flint plan on sticking around. So, tell me, what's it like to see a real fairy, a serpent, and a ghost?"

Mike looked over his shoulder and could see that Nadia was coming back inside. "Mr. Clark, I can't talk about that right now, but let me just say I don't ever think I'll ever be the same. You just get yourself back safely, and we'll see you soon. Bye now."

Before Mike hung up, Nadia rushed in, and motioned to Mike that she wanted to speak to Ethan. "Oh, wait Mr. Clark, Nadia, has something she wants to ask you."

Nadia grabbed the receiver and brushed some of the loose hairs from her bun away from her face. "Mr. Clark, I need to let you know that I've become rather close with tall Karl. Well, as a matter of fact, more than close; we are in love. And since you now have Victoria and Eric living here, would you mind if I move in with him. Victoria is a wonderful cook, and she insists on doing it. You must understand, I have fully enjoyed being part of you and Julie's lives, but I'm no longer a spring chicken as they say."

Ethan warmly replied, "Nadia. I'm awfully glad for you and Karl. I wouldn't want to stand in the way of your happiness. After all, you have given so much to me and my family. Please go ahead with your plans, and if all goes well, I'll see you all very soon."

Now that Ethan had been given the news of Nadia and the boys leaving, he began to wonder if he had made a mistake moving to the states. He thought if it were possible, he would bring everybody back to England before Jasper's exit time. However, he realized this monumental task couldn't be pulled off so fast. Instead, Ethan decided to wait and see what the serpent had in mind.

22

The rest of the week progressed, and everybody went about their business. Currently, Foster was busy in the vegetable garden giving all the grapes close inspection. Faye was working below him removing the small, dried twigs off the vines.

Foster jumped down next to Faye. "Say, I had another dream; do you want to hear about it?"

Faye leaned her head back, wearing half a smile. "Another poppy-infused dream? Or something more standard, like you're walking around naked and can't find your pants?"

Foster smiled at her reply, and then his face took on a more serious look. "No. It was about us leaving the earth plane, and the destruction of this planet. There was a great war, and many souls perished, both human and animal. I awoke saddened but was grateful that you were lying next to me. I truly hope none of this comes to pass. Nevertheless, I don't want to be around if it does."

Faye's curious expression changed to a frozen stare. "I, too, have had this feeling that we will be leaving soon. This place is wonderful, but I still miss England. Nevertheless, we have work to finish here, and then we can transition to the next level and join the rest of our kind." The two fairies embraced each other, and with their eyes closed, lay their heads on each other's shoulder.

Later that afternoon, Nadia arrived at the train station, and parked the car. She spotted Julie immediately and tooted the horn twice. Julie hurried over to the car, and got in. "Hi Nadia, I'm glad to be off that train. So, what's new?"

"Well, Julie, I have some good news, and some bad news. I spoke to your father this morning, and he says he might be able to fly out this coming Friday. Good news, right? Here's the bad. Karl and I plan to move in together, and maybe even get married. Therefore, I've made plans to leave you and your father.

Nadia was excited but looked over at Julie with a sad face. Julie reacted in much the same way, happy to have her father to come home but sad about Nadia leaving.

Julie replied, "I'm happy for you guys, and I certainly understand, Nadia. Since you've been such big part of our lives for some time now, you'll be sorely missed."

"Yes, Julie, and I've enjoyed every day of it, but it's time for me to spread my wings, and I'm not getting any younger. Besides, I told Victoria I would still be happy to continue bringing you back and forth to the station. Now, enough about me; how are things going with you and Flint?"

Julie gazed skyward out the window. "Well, we really haven't had much time to spend together. I like Flint very much, but my grandmother isn't exactly promoting our union and perhaps she's right."

Nadia half-heartily shook her head. "Julie, I come from a quite different background than you. In my small village, if a man could provide for himself, is faithful, and you are both in love, that's enough. I understand what your grandmother is talking about. Julie, you are young and should take one day at a time. What will be, will be."

Julie looked back at Nadia, and smiled, "See, this is why I'm going to miss you." They both shed a few tears of happiness and laughed at the same time.

23

Thursday morning arrived, bringing a cool nip in the air. The tops of the trees were showing more color, and the grass had finally ceased to grow so fast. Ryan, Marco, and Nadia, all planned that this would be their last week on the estate.

Jasper knew that next Monday would be the full moon, and at three o'clock his portal would close to this earth plane forever. He decided to take a walk and meet the crew for the morning huddle. Once he arrived, Jasper assumed that everybody must be inside the greenhouse. The golf cart was also parked near the front door, which meant Eric must be with them too.

Jasper pushed open the greenhouse door, and the lively conversation that was taking place came to a quick halt.

Eric turned to address Jasper. "Good morning, Jasper! I was just congratulating these two brave young men for their willingness to serve their country. It's my intention this morning to give them a nice send off. I would like to treat everybody for breakfast at the local diner. You're welcome to join us Jasper."

Jasper knew he really wouldn't be welcome, and replied, "Man, I woke up with the chickens this morning, and already had my breakfast. Thanks, but y'all go have a good time. I just ask that you be back by ten o'clock, because

I've got a project for Flint and Mike."

Flint and Mike quickly glanced at each other. Eric nodded and replied. "Oh, sure Jasper, we won't be long."

Everyone resumed their conversation and filed out the door. King hadn't noticed that everyone had left. He woke up, and saw Jasper standing before him. King sat up, looked at the door, and then back to him. Feeling an uncanny vibe, King made a quick dash out of the greenhouse.

Jasper was now alone, but he couldn't help feeling that something or someone else was in the room. He looked about the walls until his eyes stopped at two small figures looking down at from a high shelf. Foster and Faye peered down at him with stern looks on their faces.

Faye was the bravest of the two and spoke first. "We felt it was time for us to become better acquainted, and also to let you know that we thoroughly disapprove of your intentions."

Foster put his arm around Faye and held her tighter against him. "Yes! You have no right to separate Julie from her family. What are you thinking?"

Jasper stepped back. "So, what do we have here? A couple of wee creatures of the woods. No doubt you are friends with that overgrown eel. I really don't care what you think, and like I told Mr. Martin, you better stay out of my way!"

Faye leaned forward. "On the contrary, if you think you can go through with this, you're sadly mistaken. We will do whatever is in our power to stop this. As a matter of fact, I think you are outnumbered. Perhaps you should consider what you're up against, and just leave this family alone."

"Don't threaten me! Nobody is going to stop me. Nobody!" Jasper turned and walked out, slamming the door behind him.

Foster and Faye jumped back from the loud noise. They

both looked at each other, and Foster said, "You know, I think we succeeded in pushing a couple of his buttons."

Faye replied, "He may have the power to change into whatever he wants, but beyond that he's just another scared and lonely man. Let's go see Emily and remind her to hover by Julie when she gets home."

"Good idea dear, but why don't you just go? I don't know – those dolls – they just creep me out."

"Very well poppy head. While I'm gone, go make yourself useful and brew us some coffee. I'll be back soon." Faye then dashed out and ran down the hill to the playhouse.

A couple hours had passed, and the crew returned from the diner. Jasper was sitting on the wicker couch in front of the main house porch. Jasper stood up and greeted them. "Y'all enjoy your vittles?"

Eric stepped forward. "We had a good time Jasper. Wish you would have joined us. Listen Jasper, I need to steal Marco and Ryan again for one more day. We're just about finished with the cabin job."

"No problem Eric, I have a project for Mike and Flint this afternoon. The day is flying by, so if you two would follow me down to the bath house." Jasper turned and started walking down the path. Mike gave Flint a quick look and raised his eyebrows.

They followed behind Jasper, and then King appeared from the bushes and trailed after Flint and Mike.

Jasper stopped by the edge of the pool and turned facing Flint and Mike. He remained quiet for a few seconds and looked at them both. "Guys. I'm afraid I've got a problem."

Flint darted a look at Mike, and then back at Jasper. He tensed, fearing what Jasper was about to say and thought for sure the secret was out. Jasper looked over at the pool, and back at Mike and Flint. "We have to clean and shut down this pool for the season. I haven't a clue on how to execute that program. I'm counting on you guys to figure it out, and get it done. Are you up for the challenge?"

Both Mike and Flint were seriously relieved that Jasper didn't go where they anticipated. Mike shook his head. "I believe we can handle this one, Jasper. I used to have an above-ground pool, so it can't be too much different. I'm fairly sure there are some manuals somewhere inside the bath house."

"Well, good. I knew you guys would be able to figure it out. Oh, by the way, Nadia is moving in with Karl next week. Plus, with the other guys joining the service, this place is going to be quiet next week. Judging by the number of leaves on the trees, you guys got your work cut out for you."

Jasper completed that assessment and gave them one of his crescent-moon smiles. He then walked back up towards the main house.

King watched Jasper leave as he moved over to Flint and nudged his side. Flint knelt beside King and gave him a couple long dog-hugs.

Flint then looked up at Mike. "That bastard thinks he's got everything all sewed up. Little does he know; Martin has a plan. What do you think that is, Mike?"

"I don't know kid, and frankly I'm not really sure what our part in all this is. The best you and I could do is hit Jasper over the head with shovel. Guess we'll have to leave it up to these creatures and their special powers. There really isn't anything else we can do."

Mike focused back to the task. "Let's see, why don't you hook up that vacuum, and start cleaning the pool liner? I'll go see if the manuals are inside the bath house."

Flint started cleaning the pool, and while doing so, he gave some thought to what things would be like without the other guys around. He recalled what Marco told him about being accepted into the Clark family. The comments Victoria made also caused doubt about his future, and what he should do with his life. So many choices of professions to choose from, but nothing felt right except creating and playing music. Flint looked at King sleeping in the sun, and wished he were a dog and could do the same.

Later, Mike and Flint were finishing up with the pool when Julie arrived on the scene. Immediately she and Flint locked eyes. Mike observed this and elbowed to Flint. "Why don't you guys take a short walk – I don't mind."

Flint stopped what he was doing, and motioned Julie over to him. The two gave each other a quick kiss and left in the direction of the pond.

They walked out to the gazebo and took a seat inside. Flint asked, "Julie, I wish we could spend more time together, and maybe go hiking again sometime soon."

Julie hesitated for a moment, and replied, "I know, things are so crazy right now. I'll feel better when my father returns, and we can get my grandmother to relax about the two of us. I really do wish the same as you, but this is the way it must be for now. I hope you understand." Julie and Flint stared into each other's eyes, embraced, and passionately kissed each other.

At the same time, Victoria was on the back patio of the main house, observing the two from a distance. She wasn't the only one either. Jasper was in his frog form, floating several feet from the edge of the gazebo. He too, didn't approve of them kissing. Seeing this for the first-time fueled Jasper's anger even more. He submerged back into the water, and quickly swam back to his layer. He planned to transform back and walk to the gazebo to break things up between them.

At the same time, Victoria walked down to the bath house and called for Julie. In a short amount of time, both Jasper and she arrived simultaneously.

Victoria gave a loud, yoo-hoo, and followed by calling Julie's name. Mike looked up to see both she and Jasper standing in front of the bath house.

Jasper turned to Mike, and asked, "You guys figure everything out with the pool?"

Mike was crouched by the edge of pool and then decided it would best to approach them and cover for Flint's absence. He shook the water from his hands, stood up, and walked over to them. "We certainly did, the only thing left to do is put the cover on and we are good to go."

Jasper asked, "Where is Flint?" Although, he knew exactly of Flint's whereabouts.

Mike addressed both Victoria and Jasper. "I told the kid he could have break. Flint really did a nice job cleaning the pool. I believe he took a walk over to the pond with Julie. Oh, and here they come now."

As Flint and Julie approached Victoria and Jasper, they could see the stern looks on both of their faces. Flint separated and walked over next to Mike. Victoria then smiled at Julie and grabbed her hand. She quickly escorted her back up the walk to the main house.

Julie turned back and looked at Flint, rolling her eyes while she gave him a quick wave goodbye.

Jasper watched this sweet exchange, and then approached Flint. "You've got some pair of balls hitting on the boss's daughter while he's away, especially when you're getting paid to work – not just fuck around."

Mike calmly interjected, "Hey now, I told the kid he could have a break and he deserved one. So, lighten up there, cowboy."

Not wanting to reveal his true hostility, Jasper reconsidered his approach. "Alright Flint, you simply better watch yourself around here. I can tell Victoria is not very keen on the two of you having a relationship. I, too, don't think it's a particularly good idea to be working here and swapping spit with the boss's daughter.

Jasper surveyed the pool once again. "Looks like you guys got this program just about rapped up. Finish putting the cover on the pool and have yourselves a good weekend. Flint, you better think about what I told you."

Jasper walked away and headed in the direction of the pond. Mike grabbed Flint by the back of the neck and pulled him closer to his face. "Don't listen to that bag of wind. We've only got a little while longer of dealing with that son-of-a-bitch."

Flint shook his head and agreed with Mike. But one thought crossed Flint's mind. When did Jasper ever see him kiss Julie? Somehow, he must have seen them before coming to the bath house. This thought disturbed him even more, knowing that Jasper could be lurking anywhere when least expected.

24

The end of the day had arrived, and everybody convened in the driveway in front of the main house. Handshakes and best wishes were exchanged to both the boys leaving for the service. Marco made it a point to give Nadia and Julie a hug and a wink. Some small talk continued for a while longer, and then the phone rang from inside the house.

Nadia was the first to hear it and ran into the house to answer. Several minutes passed, and she opened the door and motioned for Eric to come inside. He excused himself, and as he approached Nadia, he saw that she had a solemn look on her face. She held out the receiver. "Eric, it's Mr. Clark. I'm afraid it's more bad news."

Eric nodded his head, and whispered to Nadia, "Stay inside until I talk to Ethan. Let me see what's going on before we tell the others. He took a seat at the kitchen table and picked up the receiver, "Hello Ethan, what 's going on with you?"

Ethan explained. "Unfortunately, there has been another terrorist attack. This time a truck wired with explosives went off in a parking lot, and quite a few people have been injured. As a result, all flights have once again been canceled."

Julie walked inside and asked Nadia who was on the

phone. Nadia whispered, "It's your father." Julie could see by the look on her grandfather's face, that it wasn't good news. She sat down at the table and waited quietly, wearing a worried look on her face.

Eric shook his head, and then looked Julie in the eyes. "Yes Ethan, I understand. Julie is right here in front of me. Let me put her on."

Eric handed the receiver to Julie and made a quick dash into the bathroom. At the same time, Nadia walked back outside.

Julie, quickly put the receiver to her ear. "Hello, dad! What's wrong? Are you coming home?"

"I'm not sure honey. There has been more terrorist activity, and it's preventing me from leaving. This is unbelievable. How are you? What's going on with Jasper?"

Julie replied quietly, "He seems to be leaving me alone, and everybody's been very protective. I was so hoping you were going to be here, but it doesn't look good, does it?

Ethan exhaled loudly, "No, there aren't any flights leaving anytime soon. All this seems so unbelievable. Lately, I've been feeling this move was a big mistake. As a matter of fact, with most of the crew leaving and Nadia moving in with Karl, I'm considering selling the place and having you all come back. It turns out that Ian's father and mother recently passed away, and he's looking to sell his parents' house. It's a lovely little place, and there would enough room for us and your grandparents. I know this sounds crazy, but I'm only looking out for your safety. I'm sure we can find a similar program that you can transfer to in England. Anyway, these are just some ideas I've been toying with. We'll see, Julie. For now, please have Mike call me next week, or certainly before then if anything should happen."

Julie's head was spinning from what her father had just proposed, but she understood his reasoning. "Dad, whatever you want to do is fine with me, but perhaps things will work out."

"Alright Julie, but I'm giving this idea some more thought. In the meantime, please keep me informed. I don't care what time of the day it is. Ian is aware of my situation, and he's ready to answer the phone at any time. I love you, and I know everything will work out one way or another. Just relax; we'll be together again real soon. Take care, Julie."

By this time, Eric had returned outside and had announced Ethan's predicament to everybody. Marco spit on the ground and was about to spew some descriptive words but remembered he had better watch his tongue given the present company. Flint and Mike gave each other a brief concerned stare. Nadia embraced Victoria, and Jasper pretended to wear a concerned look on his face, but inside he was reveling in this news.

Eric raised his arms and got everybody's attention again. "This is disheartening news, I know, but we must all remain positive and be thankful that Ethan is safe and well. He'll be back soon; I'm sure of this. Let's all relax and have a good weekend. Marco and Ryan, I'm enormously proud of you. Go and give those bastards hell but get your asses back in one piece."

Everyone dispersed, the crew left for home, and the family walked back into the main house. Jasper was left standing alone. He was about to turn and leave when he saw Emily sitting in the wicker couch. She gave him a smile and gestured with her two fingers by pointing them at her eyes, and then pointing back at him. This was to ensure Jasper that she was keeping her eyes on him. He just made a huffing noise and walked down the driveway to the gatehouse.

That evening, everyone remained rather quiet in the main house. Eric, Victoria, and Nadia stayed glued to the television and watched all the news reports. Julie decided she had enough news for the evening, so she grabbed Polly and went upstairs to lay in her bed. Julie wasn't totally against moving back to England. Getting situated into another school was the least of her worries. However, not being able to continue seeing Flint was her biggest concern. Feeling doubtful, the thought crossed her mind that their relationship wasn't exactly going the way she had hoped it would, either. The conflicting views of her grandmother, coupled with the lack of time they could spend together, caused Julie to burst into tears. Polly sensed Julie's sadness and crawled next her and purred loudly. Polly's comfort seemed to work for Julie, and within a few minutes she fell fast asleep.

Later that evening, Flint partied with Marco, Ryan, and a few other local friends. Everyone proceeded to get polluted, as Mike would put it.

Flint couldn't help feeling a bit left out of the 'fight for your country' vibe. It wasn't that he didn't care about the attacks on innocent people. He too was outraged about what was happening. The fact was that he had other plans for his life, and if he had a choice, dying in battle wasn't one of them. After all, Flint was already fighting his own battle with Jasper.

Marco noticed Flint wasn't having as good a time, so he moved face to face with him. "You've got to get over the idea that you're going to make it with Julie. She's a rich girl who has her whole life already sewn up. You're just living from paycheck to paycheck. Water seeks its own level, and brother you are way below sea level. You understand what I'm saying? There's plenty of fish in the sea. Get over it and have another beer."

Marco's polluted peep talk didn't fill Flint with much confidence, but he did take his advice and had another beer. For the remainder of the evening, Flint decided to forget about everything and try to have a good time.

On the other side of the Atlantic, Ethan had begun to give serious thought about bringing everybody back to England. Selling the property might be a challenge, but Ian's house was there waiting for them. The increasing incidents forced Ethan to seriously consider this decision, and the sooner the better.

25

I t was a chilly Monday morning, and Flint and Mike arrived at the estate a bit earlier than normal. They went inside the greenhouse and leaned against the counter while they sipped their coffee. It was apparent that the room was quiet without Marco and Ryan present.

Mike abruptly broke the silence. "I don't know about you kid, but today just doesn't feel the same. According to Martin, today is the full moon, and this is the day Jasper's supposed to return. Somehow, we must make sure he doesn't end up taking Julie with him. I don't know about you, but I really wish we knew what to do about all this."

Flint replied, "Guess we should make sure we stay close to the main house when Julie gets home. Maybe before three o'clock one of us should take the golf cart to the beginning of the driveway and follow her back."

"That's a good idea, kid. I'll tell Jasper the mailbox needs to be cleared of some hanging tree limbs. This will give us an excuse to split up."

Both Mike and Flint's attention was redirected by the sound of a faint call coming from the top shelf. Both fairies were calling down to them. "Good morning!"

Foster and Faye jumped down to get closer to Flint and Mike. Mike hunched down with his hands on his knees and moved closer to them. "Me and kid are still in limbo on how we're supposed to save Julie. What do you guys have planned?"

Faye smiled back. "Despite his malicious intentions, Jasper has some fragile weaknesses that we may be able use to our advantage. The other day Foster and I stood up to him by displaying no fear. By doing this, he grew flustered and backed down. I think he knows he's outnumbered.

Mike stood back up and scratched the back of head. "You're probably right. Flint and I have come up with a plan to make sure Julie at least gets safely back to the house."

Suddenly, the greenhouse door burst open, causing Foster and Faye to quickly dart for cover. Victoria entered wearing a large, floppy garden-hat. Fortunately, the brim of her hat hung in front of her eyes enough to obscure her view of the two fairies scurrying for cover.

Victoria looked up and smiled. "You're just the two I was hoping find this morning. Do you think you both could assist me in planting some mums behind the main house?"

Mike returned a smile. "Yes, of course, but you'll need to go to the nursery, right? The kid, I mean Flint, and I will first have to clean out those beds of all the summer plantings. While we're busy getting the flower beds ready, I suggest you find Jasper and see if he can give you a ride." Mike finished and winked at Flint.

Momentarily pausing, Victoria uttered, "Oh, why you're right, Mike. Yes. Splendid idea! We will need to prepare the beds first. I'll go fetch Jasper."

Once she was well on her way, Faye and Foster reappeared. With a twinkle in her eyes, Faye looked up at Mike. "Bravo my good man. That was a brilliant idea to get both her and Jasper out of our hair for a spell."

Faye turned to Foster. "Now, poppy head, why don't you

gather Emily, and we'll all meet down by the pond in fifteen minutes. Maybe Martin has something he can tell
us."

"Yes dear." Foster reluctantly replied.

Flint gathered a couple
shovels and the tree cutters
and loaded them into the
wheelbarrow outside the
door. He was beside himself
worrying about how this
whole escapade was going to
unfold. Without acknow-
ledging the others, he
started pushing the wheelbarrow down the driveway.
The other three watched him leave and looked at each
other in silent reverence.

Walking behind Flint, Mike followed with a drop cloth
slung over his shoulders. Faye had perched herself inside
one of the folds of the drop cloth, which gave her a good
view of the road ahead.

With one arm Mike pulled a cigarette from shirt pocket
and stuck it the corner of his mouth. He then stopped and
watched Flint slowly walk down the driveway. Mike lit
the *Pall Mall*, took a deep inhale, and blew the smoke up
into the trees. He thought to himself, this whole situation
just isn't fair to such a young kid.

Mike took another drag and spit on the ground. He whispered, "I'll be glad when this whole thing is over and done
with." Faye silently nodded in agreement.

Back at the gatehouse, Jasper had just stepped out of the
shower and was standing before the mirror in his natural
state. His frogs head was now proportional to his human
body. Jasper's body resembled that of a normal human

being, except that his toes and fingers were slightly webbed. He was satisfied with his own physique, but feared Julie wouldn't find him attractive. Even though Jasper had the power to change into anyone, he still hoped Julie would eventually accept his natural form. Knowing today was the day he would bring Julie back to his watery domain, a sinister smile slowly began to grow on his face.

Unheard by Jasper, Victoria rolled in front of the gate-house in the golf cart. She whisked herself out of the seat and knocked on the garage door. Startled by the intrusion, he quickly grabbed his bathrobe and hurried down the stairs to see who was there.

With each step, he reverted to the form everybody was accustomed to. Before arriving at the door, he saw Victoria's face pressed close to the window, looking up through the glass.

Branding a large smile, Jasper opened the door, and said, "Good Morning, what brings you here?"

Victoria was embarrassed to see him wearing his bath-robe. She eyed him from head to foot, and for some odd reason she couldn't take her eyes off his feet.

At that very moment, she noticed Jasper's toes were spaced wider apart than normal, and they were also webbed. She caught herself, and didn't want to be rude, so she quickly returned her attention to his face. "Hi Jasper, I'm deeply sorry to have caught you at such a bad time, and I apologized for the intrusion.

"No worries. Well, you're certainly the early bird." replied Jasper. The rest of his body was now fully morphed to normal, and he was perplexed why she was there.

Victoria nervously blurted out. "Jasper, I have a project that Mike and Flint are helping me with, and I need a ride to the nursery to purchase some chrysanthemums. I know this is unexpected, but it would only take a few minutes. Would you mind taking me there? You see, Eric is busy with the plumbing project in the cabin, and I..."

Jasper held up both his hands. "I'd be glad to. Just give me five minutes to get dressed, and I'll be down in two shakes of a nanny goat's tail."

Victoria shook her head, and shot a quick look at Jasper's feet again, but they had returned to normal. "Why thank you my dear man, do take your time. Again, I apologize."

Victoria walked back to the golf cart and sat down. She couldn't stop thinking about Jasper's feet changing like that. However, she quickly attributed the anomaly to the morning sun streaming in from behind her. Before contemplating it any further, Jasper burst from the door and joyfully announced, "Let's go!"

Foster was now on his way to see Emily. He left from the greenhouse and cut through the woods. After dodging a couple of chipmunks, he finally arrived at the playhouse.

The door was closed, but as soon as he stepped in front of it, the door opened. Foster walked into the playroom and called for Emily. "Halloo, anybody home? It's me, Foster! Emily, are you here?"

Just then, a strong breeze came from above his head. Emily passed through the top of the roof and floated down before him. With bulging eyes, she looked down. "Hey you. Guess what? I just got back from Saturn. That is, I didn't walk on the planet, but rather I floated nearby, and checked out its rings. They were beautiful!" It felt like I was on-board the Jupiter 2 with the Robinson family. It is a silly show, but I really enjoyed it. How about you?"

Baffled again by these human entertainment references, Foster cast his eyes down and back at Emily. "Noooo. I'm here to have you join everybody down at the pond. Were all hoping to contact Martin and hopefully get some information on what we're supposed to do."

"Yeah, that Jasper sure is strange. I wish he would just go home and leave Julie alone. So, silly, let's get going. We don't want to be late for the party." Emily shrunk herself to the size of Foster, grabbed his hand, and the two made their way down to the pond.

Within a short time, everyone had convened at the gazebo at the south end of the pond. Inside the octagonal structure, there were built-in benches beneath each window. Everyone was seated and waiting for Martin's arrival.

After a few minutes, everyone's attention was drawn to a bright-green, cylindrical-light protruding from the middle of the floor. Following the light, Martin's head and a small section of his body was visible.

He announced, "I'm awfully glad you are all here. You're probably wondering what the plan is, and how you can assist. That is admirable indeed, but only I can deal with Jasper. You must allow Julie to be captured by Jasper. That sounds preposterous, I know, but it will have to happen. He will need to bring her into the water for me to intervene. Timing is of the utmost importance."

Wearing a frown, Faye interjected, "I don't know if I can just stand around and watch that happen. Can't we all drop a tree on him or something."

Mike and Flint looked at each other and shook their heads in agreement. Foster started pounding his fist on the seat. At the same time, Emily started swirling around the ceiling of the gazebo.

Martin closed his eyes, shook his head, and raised his voice. "Now stop!! All of you! This family is my responsibility, and even if Ethan was here, I'm the only one who can take care of this matter. This I will do, but it will have to be done alone!"

Martin relaxed and continued. "Now, please forgive me for raising my voice. You must know that I'm immensely proud and grateful for your concern. This burden is a heavy one. And Flint, gallant as you may be, you are no match for this creature. As a matter of fact, none of you are. Just keep going about your business, and it will all work out fine."

Martin fixed his gaze at the floor and lowered his voice. "There is one thing I will need for you to do. If my calculations are correct, his portal will close just a few moments past the hour. Therefore, I will need you all to be waiting at the stone bridge at that precise moment. You will need to be standing ready to pull Julie from the water. That is all you need to know, and I have all the confidence in the world in each one of you. Goodbye for now and wish me the best."

A bright, green colored flash of light filled the entire gazebo, and Martin disappeared. Everyone sat silently, with beguiled looks on their faces.

Flint and Mike returned to preparing the flower beds for Victoria's plantings. Foster, Faye, and Emily made their way back up through the brush.

Once they reached the playhouse, Emily smiled at the two fairies. "Come on, you guys, Martin's gonna save the day; we know he is. He's Puff the Magic Dragon! Well, you know what I mean."

Both the fairies looked at each other and shrugged their shoulders. Faye shook her head in agreement. "Alright Emily, you're probably right.

"Of course, she is." Foster replied. "Let's go settle our nerves with a cup of tea."

Faye gave him a stern sideways glance. "My tea, not

yours."
  Foster replied, "Yes dear. Whatever you wish."

26

The rest of the morning painfully crept along. The turning of the flower beds was now complete and ready for Victoria's chrysanthemums.

Mike and Flint were seated in the chairs on the back patio. Both stopped talking when they heard Jasper's truck pulling in front of the main house. They could also hear Victoria's chatty voice echoing from the other side of the house.

Jasper continued to agree with Victoria, replying with simple, one-word answers. The two rounded the side of the house both carrying pots of mums in each hand. They set them down, and Victoria instantly put her hands together and joyfully exclaimed, "What a wonderful job the two of you have done!" Both Flint and Mike smiled and nodded their heads.

Before they could reply, Jasper interrupted, "Say, you guys wanna go around the front and bring the rest of the mums 'round back."

The two passed Jasper and threw him a neutral look. Jasper and Victoria remained behind the house and continued to chit-chat about how the mums were going to be arranged.

On the other side of the house, Flint tapped Mike on the shoulder and pointed to his watch. "Say, it's just a little past two o'clock. Nadia should be bringing Julie back in about twenty minutes. I still think you should go up to the mailbox and …"

Mike interrupted Flint. "No, that doesn't matter now, besides, Queen-Bee is gonna want us to put those mums in the ground. So, we better stick around."

"Yeah, your right." agreed Flint.

Just at that moment, Jasper rounded the corner, and gave Flint a stone-faced stare. "Say Flint, I really hate to lay this on you, but that chicken coup sure needs to be cleaned again. Since Ryan and Marco aren't around anymore, some things just got pushed to the back burner. I'd really appreciate if you'd get on that."

Mike gave Flint a reassuring glance, and said, "Go ahead kid, I'll take care of the plantings."

Once the truck was fully emptied, Jasper jumped in and took off towards the gatehouse. Upon arriving, he saw that the golf cart was still parked in front. Knowing that Eric would appreciate having it back, he decided to go and return it. This way Jasper would have all his ducks in a row when three o'clock rolled around. Jasper hopped in the golf cart and took off for the cabin.

When Jasper arrived at the cabin, it caused King to awaken from his nap. Seeing that it was Jasper, King let out a few loud barks. Eric heard King barking and stepped out outside. "Oh, it's only you Jasper. King! Stop with the barking!" Eric insisted.

After giving King a stink-eye, Jasper turned his attention back to Eric. "Say, thought you might want this little buggy back?"

Once again, King started barking again at Jasper. Mimicking a monster, Jasper raised both his arms abruptly, and lunged towards King. Though Jasper only appeared harmless in front of Eric; King, knew otherwise. He gave one more bark and then started running back to the main house, hoping to find Polly. Eric just laughed, thanked Jasper, and walked back inside the cabin.

Jasper wasn't in the mood for idol chit-chat either, so he started walking back to the main drive. King was already a couple hundred yards ahead of Jasper. He looked back once and hurried out of sight.

Jasper was almost to the stone bridge when, suddenly, Emily materialized several feet in front of him. Startled by her appearance, Jasper stopped and peered down at Emily. Slowly, Jasper began to morph into his natural appearance.

Emily swallowed a lump in her throat but stood her ground. She snidely replied, "I'm not afraid of you. Furthermore, I think you should just dive in that water and leave us in peace. You have no right to break up this family. Julie is not in love with you, and she never will be. So, just leave. NOW!"

Jasper was enraged by her tone, and at the same time hurt by the sobering reminder that Julie wasn't in love with him. He didn't reply to this but instead closed his eyes.

From the center of his forehead emerged a series of three, silver-glowing triangles, starting out small but changing in size. Jasper positioned them just above Emily's head.

Confused, Emily looked up at them, but before she could move, the rings dropped around her ankles, midsection, and neck. Emily was now frozen where she hovered. Her eyes looked back in rage at Jasper, but he quickly rendered her in a state of suspended animation. Emily was now unable to speak or move.

Jasper was able to control the triangles and positioned her high atop one of the trees above the bridge. Emily was helpless as she watched Jasper shrink to a bullfrog and jump into the water.

With Emily contained, he proceeded to revitalize his powers in preparation for his final exit.

Julie had caught the express from Grand Central and was on her way home. Her thoughts were a merry-go-round of emotions. A wave of exhaustion overcame her, and she soon feel asleep. A half-hour had passed when the train conductor opened the door and made the final call. "Croton-Harmon Station, this way out!"

Julie awoke just in time to grab her backpack and quickly run off the train before it lurched forward. She gathered herself and dashed through the depot and then out to the parking lot.

Nadia was already standing against the car, shaking both of her hands to get Julie's attention. They both quickly embraced and left the station.

They hurried back to the estate and the station wagon parked in front of the main house. Julie stepped out of the car and onto the front porch. Both King and Polly were sitting on the wicker couch. She leaned down and gave them both a quick pat on the head and opened the door. Before she entered, the two animals bounded in front of her, causing Julie to temporarily lose her balance. "Hey! What gives?" She yelled.

Before Julie arrived home, King and Polly had been discussing their concern for the family and what to do about Jasper. Because of their concern, they wanted to hang close to Julie.

Julie put her book bag down and called out. "Hello! Grandmother, are you home?!"

A faint voice came from the back of the house. "Julie! I'm in the back, come outside." Victoria opened the back door, and repeated. "Back here dear, come see the pretty chrysanthemums!"

King and Polly followed behind Julie, but she closed the door on them as she left the house. King sulked and proceeded to watch Julie's every move. Polly stood frozen for a moment but then darted back to the kitchen to chow on some kibble.

Julie praised Victoria for her choice in color and commented on the clever arrangement of the plantings.

Victoria stood staring at her creation. "Oh, thank you dear. They are wonderful, but I'm dirty and in need of a shower. I also need to get dinner started soon. Would you like to give me a hand in a little while?"

Before answering, Julie peered down at the gazebo and nodded. "Sure. But while you're cleaning up, I'm going to stretch my legs, and take little walk."

Victoria ripped the soiled gloves off her hands. Her demeanor changed slightly, and she replied, "Certainly dear, I'll see you shortly."

Julie knew why her grandmother's attitude changed, but she wasn't going to allow her to influence her decisions. She smiled and touched her grandmother on the shoulder. "I'll see you soon."

Julie cut through the tall rhododendron bushes and then down the slate pathway to the bath house. She surveyed the distant grounds hoping to spot Flint. Not seeing any sign of him, she continued over to the gazebo and took a seat inside.

A soft breeze blew through the screened-in porch, and the sound of distant chainsaws buzzed in the distance.

Julie heard a tiny splash from behind her. She turned and looked but saw nothing. When she turned back around, there standing before her was Flint. He smiled and apologized for sneaking up on her. Julie's heart melted. She stood up, and they embraced.

Julie looked back at the main house and then returned her attention to Flint. "I've been thinking about you and many other things."

Flint glanced back up to the house, and replied, "Yeah, me too. I really shouldn't be here right now. Jasper has me cleaning the chicken coup again, but I needed a break. So, I decided to sneak away and see if you were home. Let's take a walk, and you can tell me what's on your mind."

Flint and Julie started following the edge of the pond and passed before the main house. At that moment, Victoria stepped out of the shower and peered down through the window to see them walking together.

She couldn't help feeling that Julie was making a big mistake growing so attached to this young man. She wished it would end so Julie could put all her attention into school. Nevertheless, she didn't want to meddle but decided she wasn't going to hold her tongue when it came time to discuss this with Ethan.

Meanwhile, up in the attic section of the greenhouse, Faye and Foster were fast asleep napping after their tea. Faye's eyes opened, and she suddenly realized the time. She sat straight up and gave Foster a hard elbow against his shoulder. "Wake up! It's almost three o'clock! We need to gather the others!"

Springing out of bed with his eyes half closed, Foster exuded a groan and slipped on his shoes. The two of them scurried like a pair of mice down from the attic. As they exited out of the greenhouse, they saw Mike coming up the driveway pushing a wheelbarrow full of tools.

Mike was also aware of the time and spotted the two of them standing together. He stretched his neck looking in both directions and then crouched down to the fairies. "Say, we've got to get everyone together. You find Emily, and I'll go get Flint."

With a curious look, Faye inquired, "Where is Flint? I thought he was working with you?"

Mike looked over his shoulder and turned back. "No. Jasper made him clean the chicken coup again. Poor kid."

I'll go get him. With a stern stare, he looked back at both fairies. "We still have about ten minutes. Flint and I will see you guys at the bridge. But remember, stay hidden from sight."

"Alright Mike." replied Foster. "See you soon."

By this time, Julie and Flint had walked to the other end of the pond. They were only a couple yards from the stone bridge when they heard a loud bang that sounded like it came from the cabin.

Julie looked over, and said, "That must be Grandpa Eric. Why don't we go say hello! Alright?"

Flint replied, "Sure, alright." They slowly walked in the direction of the cabin until they came to the middle of the bridge.

Flint stopped and put both his hands-on Julie's shoulders. He leaned forward, pulled her close to his body, and started kissing her.

Julie was warmed at first, but her body began to grow cold, which caused her eyes to slowly open. To her dismay, the man kissing her was no longer Flint. Instead, it was Jasper's face she was looking back at.

Julie attempted to back away but found herself unable to speak or move. The look on Jasper's face was filled with disappointment by her reaction. As he stood before her, his face began to change into his natural form.

Julie's face turned white with horror from the sight of this strange looking, frog-like creature.

Jasper quietly spoke, "I'm sorry if my true appearance disgusts you, but in time you will grow to like it. If it pleases you, I can be whoever you want. Whatever you choose, it really makes no difference. The important thing is that you will be with me. Forever."

Julie couldn't believe what was happening and she wondered where everyone else was, especially Martin.

From the center of Jasper's forehead, came a glowing purple light that encapsulated them both. He then levitated the purple cocoon about two feet off the ground, suspended it over the pond, and plunged it into the water below.

Once they contacted the water, the cocoon burst. Jasper then grasped Julie's arm, and started rapidly swimming to the entrance of his portal. The only person witnessing this was Emily. She was still helplessly stuck at the top of the tree, bound by the three glowing triangle restraints.

On the other side of the property, Mike burst open the chicken coup door, and yelled, "Put that shovel down Kid, we've gotta go!"

They both ran as fast as they could down to the stone bridge. From out of nowhere, Faye and Foster appeared from behind Mike and Flint. They all approached the bank of pond nearly falling in from the velocity of their pace.

At that moment, Emily was able to break free from her restraints. She called down to them, "He's got Julie, they're under the water!"

Everyone peered down at water, but only a few small ripples of water rocked against the banks of the pond. Helplessly, they all remained stunned about what to do.

Flint was about to drive in the water, but Mike restrained him from doing so. "No kid, remember what Martin said; you are no match against this creature."

Flint momentarily lunged towards the pond and cursed Jasper. The rest gathered next to him, and they continued to stare at the water below, anticipating some sign of Julie or Martin.

Underneath the water, Jasper held Julie tightly as they floated at the entrance of the portal. He reveled that he had accomplished his task and was about to have Julie for his very own. The circular rock began to become transparent, and Jasper pulled them through to the other side.

Jasper was now standing on the other side and holding tightly onto Julie's wrist. He was instantly caught off guard by the sound of a large splash, followed by a flash of green light.

In one swift motion, Martin spiraled completely out of the water, and slapped Jasper in the face with his tail fin. This caused Jasper to release his grip on Julie. Within a split-second, Martin once more wrapped his tailfin around Julie, and immediately flung her back through the portal.

Now back in the pond, disoriented and frightened for her life, Julie used every bit of her strength and started swimming upwards. She burst at the top with a loud splash and gasped for her breath.

To everyone's amazement, and just as Martin had promised, Julie appeared.

Mike and Flint quickly ran into the water and helped her back onto the bank. Julie coughed out some water and caught her breath. In shock, and still trembling from the chilly water, she lunged forward and embraced Flint.

"What happened!" yelled Foster. "Where is Martin?"

Julie replied, "He pushed me back out, but I fear he must still be trapped on the other side with Jasper."

Faye jumped onto Julie's right shoulder and whispered into her ear. "Julie, the important thing is you are back, and we'll never have to worry about Jasper again."

Soaking wet, Julie let go of Flint and looked back at the water. "I don't know what happened to Martin. Everything happened so fast. I do hope he is alright."

Mike stared back at Julie. "That serpent knows how to take care of himself. No doubt, he's trapped wherever Jasper comes from, but I have faith he'll figure a way to get back."

Emily called to the others in a loud whisper, "Heads up! The old man is coming in the golf cart." She vanished immediately, and the fairies made a mad dash for the woods.

Julie turned, to see her grandfather approaching them. She whispered to Mike and Flint, "Let me do the talking."

Wearing a perplexed look on his face, Eric piped up, "What the devil happened to you, Julie?"

"Oh Grandpa. I was trying pick one of the waterlilies in the pond. I ended up slipping and fell completely into the water. So silly of me. Luckily, Flint and Mike were around to help me out of the water."

"Well. Let's get you home, and into something dry. By the way, thank you guys for helping. Glad you were around."

Julie got in the golf cart, and they took off for the main house. She turned back to Flint and Mike, and yelled, "Thanks again, guys!"

Mike pulled out the pack of cigarettes from in his pocket and gestured the pack to Flint. "Want one kid? I know it's not wacky tobacco, but after all that, we deserve a smoke."

"Yeah, thanks Mike, for sure. What a freaking relief. Ya' know something just crossed my mind. How are we going to explain Jasper's absence to Eric and Victoria?"

"That's simple enough. I'll tell them he got a call from Oklahoma, and he had to return due to some family crisis. Ethan will have to elaborate further by telling them he must have decided not to come back – something like that." Mike smiled back at Flint and gave him a wink.

THE SERPENT OF WOODLANDS

On the other side of the portal, Jasper stood foaming at the mouth in a fit of rage. "You dammed overgrown eel! You had no right to interfere with my plans!"

Crouched down in the water, Martin exclaimed, "I have every right to guard the family I've been assigned to. I wasn't about to stand by and let you ruin their lives." With bulging eyes, a glowing beam of light began to form from Jasper's forehead. He was fully intending to release this harmful light onto Martin. Uncertain what to expect from this, Martin was about to wrap himself around Jasper's entire body and squeeze him to oblivion.

Just at that moment, projecting from behind Martin, a translucent purple net flew past him and encapsulated Jasper, rendering him motionless. Martin backed down and turned to see three creatures like Jasper, standing several feet away. The center creature was controlling the net with an attached beam coming from his outstretched hand.

They were the same three elders Jasper had consulted with on his last visit.

The apparent leader shook his head and spoke, "Jasper. We talked about this, and instead, you went ahead and disobeyed our advice."

With a twisted look on his face, Jasper exclaimed, "I've done my time, and did everything you asked of me. I deserved to have what I wanted!"

Jasper dropped his head and stared at the ground. Slowly the twisted look on his face softened. "I really meant no harm to come to her. I would have cared and loved her with all my heart."

Martin winced his eyes and shook his head.

The elder spoke again. "Jasper, you must understand that this couldn't have been a one-sided relationship. I told you if the girl were willing, she would have been allowed. Your selflessness shall not go unpunished, but given your motives and earnest intentions, we shall go easy on you. However, let me be clear. You shall never be able to return to that dimension for as long as you exist. Do you understand?"

Jasper closed his eyes and nodded his head in acceptance. He glanced back at Martin with a look of bitter resentment. Jasper slowly became transparent and vanished all together.

The elder then directed his attention to Martin. "We apologize. You must understand; we didn't send Jasper to cause such stress to your family and friends. Your gallant efforts in stopping Jasper are very much admired. Had you not intervened; we wouldn't have been able to return the girl to her dimension. However, please understand, no harm would have ever come to her. We find you to be a magnificent creature, and we wish to extend the offer to remain here in our domain. However, I'm sure this is not your wish."

The elder tiled his head, and continued, "Unfortunately, we are unable to return you just yet. You must wait for the next full moon to exit from here. Until that time, you shall be our honored guest. Come with us now and rest in our chambers. In addition, don't concern yourself with Jasper. He has been sent to a type of detention and will be unable to leave for a short time. I promise you will have no further interaction with him while you are here."

Martin peered back at the portal opening, and wished he could return, but this wasn't meant to be. His only consolation was that Julie was now safe and unharmed. Martin rose from the water and bowed to the elder. "My dear sir, thank you for your generosity and hospitality. Therefore, I accept."

For the first time in a while, things finally felt normal for

Julie. Earlier, she helped her grandmother prepare dinner, which allowed her to deflate from the afternoon's traumatic events. Julie also received constant rubs on the leg from Polly along with some drool-laden licks on the hand from King. It had been a long, hard-working day for both Eric and Victoria. Everyone retired to a pleasant, cool, and quiet evening at the Woodlands Estate.

27

The next morning Mike knocked on the main house door. Eric had already been up and was reading the paper at the kitchen table. Eric walked over and opened the door. "Why, hello Mike. What brings you here so early? Everything alright?"

Mike slowly nodded his head, and replied, "Certainly, just wanted you to know that I passed Jasper on my way in this morning. Apparently, he just received some news from home, and was told he was needed back in Oklahoma. He apologized for having to leave so abruptly but asked me to let you know. He mentioned something to the effect about following up with Ethan when had the chance. So, that's all. You enjoy your day – I'll be around if you need me."

Eric twisted his head a little and looked up in the air. He smiled back at Mike, and said, "Oh. Alright. Thanks for letting me know. Mike, between you and me, I can't say that I'll be missing his absence."

Mike replied, "Yeah. My sentiments exactly. He gave Eric a wink and closed the door.

Eric returned to the kitchen table and was about to go back to reading the paper when the telephone rang. Realizing everybody else was still in bed, he answered it immediately. "Hello. Oh, Ethan it's you. Funny you should call. I just received some news to relate to you. It seems Jasper was called back to Oklahoma. Apparently, he had some family matter of some kind to attend to. He told Mike this and mentioned he would contact you at some point."

Ethan's first reply was, "Eric. How is Julie?"

"Julie? Oh, she's simply fine – fast asleep though. Do you want me to wake her?"

A rush of relief overcame Ethan, knowing that Martin had succeeded. He quickly answered, "No, it's not necessary, and thanks for informing me about Jasper. Perhaps it's just as well. Listen. I have some important news concerning all of you. I know this is going to come as a shock, but I've decided to move us all back to England."

Eric was taken back by this news and stated, "Well, Ethan, I'm a bit surprised to hear this. After all, Julie just started with school and Victoria and I have already done so much here. I'm confused. What's your reason, son?"

"I've given this decision much thought and realize now that I made a hasty decision. I convinced myself that this move would help me heal, start anew, and all that. However, with much of the crew and Nadia gone, we just don't need such a large place. I can pull some academic strings and arrange to have Julie transferred to a good school here in England."

Eric shook his head in agreement and replied, "I understand, Ethan. England is your home, as well as Julie's. Where do you plan on moving?"

Ethan explained. "Ian's parents recently passed, and he's looking to sell their bungalow. As a matter of fact, there is a small mother-in-law cottage on the property that would be perfect for you and Victoria. In the  long run, it would be so much easier to manage. I've already been in touch with a realtor in New York, and he's informed me that there's a young Australian couple that would love to move into the estate and take over as soon as possible."

Eric looked up to the ceiling and rubbed his forehead with one hand and replied, "You know Ethan, Victoria and I are with you no matter what you decide to do. But I fear Julie is going to be a bit upset about all this."

Ethan nodded in agreement. "I know; it's about Flint. Sadly, these things happen in our lives. I'll have a talk with her later. Tell Mike I'll need to speak to him also. Please tell Julie I love her and let her know that we'll all be back together very soon."

"Alright Ethan, I will. Bye now." Eric hung up the phone, and just stared at the floor for a few moments. He then resumed reading the paper and finishing his breakfast.

Later that afternoon, Mike, Flint, the Fairies and Emily all met down by the gazebo. They were all still hoping Martin would magically return. Overall, everyone was relieved that Jasper was gone for good, but the unknown of the serpent's well-being still concerned them.

Emily floated high above the water to get a bird's eye view of the entire pond, but there was still no sign of Martin anywhere. She returned to the gazebo and whispered down to everyone. "I think you guys should scatter; it looks like the old guy is looking for one of you."

With that alert, Foster and Faye dashed up a nearby weeping willow tree. Mike suggested to Flint for him to go to the greenhouse and bring down some rakes and drop cloths. He walked over to the bath house, and yelled, "Eric! It's me Mike. Were you looking for me?!"

Eric heard Mike calling and moved in his direction. "There you are. Hi Mike. Say, Ethan just called and wanted to speak with you. Since you weren't nearby, I thought it best to fill you in on what's going on.

They both went inside the bath house and sat down. Eric proceeded to let Mike know of Ethan's decision to move the family back to England. After a few minutes of discussion, the two men split up. Eric returned to the main house, Mike rejoined Flint, and the two went back to raking leaves.

Mike decided not to inform Flint of the family's plans, especially since he knew how much he cared for Julie. After yesterday's events Mike felt it would best to give Flint a break from all the drama. After all, he felt this bitter news would be best conveyed to Flint by Julie herself. However, Mike was eager to inform the Fairies of Ethan's decision, so he excused himself and walked up to the greenhouse.

Once Mike arrived, he went inside, sat down, and fired up a cigarette. After a few drags, he looked up at the shelf and saw Faye and Foster peering down at him.

Faye noticed a change in Mike, and asked, "What's on your mind? You look thousand miles away!"

"Well, somebody's going to be a thousand miles away – but not me. Turns out Ethan telephoned Eric and told him that he plans to bring the family back to England."

Mike elaborated, "Ethan said the estate is more than he wants to continue to take on, and apparently he already has a place to bring everyone back to. I guess I can't blame him, especially after what has just taken place. I mostly feel sorry for Julie and Flint.

Faye looked back at Foster with concern. "Yes, this will come as a surprise to them. Faye focused her attention back to Mike. "This is also a shock for us too. After all, we thought this would be our home for the remainder of our time on Earth."

Closing his eyes, Foster shook his head back and forth. "I'm not going back. I can't take that trip again! I just can't."

Foster then burst into tears, causing Faye to do the same. After a few moments they collected themselves. Then Faye looked back at Mike. "You must excuse us. We both need some time alone to process this. Thank you for your understanding."

Now reaching the end of his smoke, Mike threw it on the floor, and stamped it out. "Yes, of course. I understand. We'll talk again."

Mike exited the greenhouse and walked down the driveway. He had almost reached the main house when he heard a car door close. It was Julie saying goodbye to Nadia. To avoid making any contact with Julie, Mike stood still. It would be hard for him to conceal the information she was about to receive from her grandfather. So, he decided to wait until she went inside.

Julie let the screen door slam on her way in, which alerted Eric and Victoria that she was home. Rifling through the cabinets, she found some crackers to chase her empty stomach groans. Victoria entered the kitchen and extended her arms to her. "Julie dear! How was your day?"

Following through with the quick embrace, Julie replied, "Pretty good, but it just dragged, and none of the lessons seemed to interest me today."

A few seconds later, Eric walked in the kitchen. He smiled at Julie, but he had an urgent look on his face. "Julie dear, please have a seat. I have some important news from your father to tell you."

Still pushing more crackers in her mouth, Julie looked back with wide eyes. "What? Is father coming home?"

Eric quickly glanced at Victoria, and then back to Julie. "Well, it turns out, we are all coming... I mean, going back home. To England! Your father has concluded that this place is just too much to handle. It turns out he wants to purchase Ian's parent's home. He has already found a buyer for Woodlands and is now busy with the process of getting us all of us back to England.

Victoria excitingly stated, "Julie, we'll all be able to live together, and this house sounds lovely. Plus, your father has already arranged a transfer for you. Isn't that just wonderful?"

Wearing a deer-in-the-headlights look on her face, Julie had to allow this information to sink in. "I can't believe this! Really?!"

Her grandparents were glowing with happiness to see Julie so excited. However, Julie's expression quickly changed after realizing Flint would no longer be part of the equation.

Quick to notice the change on Julie's face, Victoria reached out, and touched Julie on the knee. "What's the matter, dear?"

Julie returned a brief smile that quickly turned to a serious stare. She then gazed out the kitchen window and asked, "But what about, Flint? I mean, we've become close."

Victoria's mouth opened, and she was ready to launch into a sobering assessment of what she felt about their relationship. However, before she did, Eric darted a stern glance at Victoria, signaling easy does it. After thirty-five years of marriage, Victoria understood her husband's look. She then reconsidered her approach.

"Julie. I understand your affection for Flint, but you are both so young. I mean, you with school and all. Besides, Flint needs to discover what he wants to do with his life. These kinds of things happen when you're young, and you both are just starting the journey of life."

With a soft tone in his voice, Eric grabbed Julie's hand, and gave it squeeze. "Honey. I understand this is hard for you, but I feel it's best for now. Your father needs us, and perhaps in time you will see Flint again. You two could write – maybe arrange a visit sometime. Be brave, and everything will be what it's meant to be in the end."

Eric pulled Julie closer, and gave her a big bear hug. "There, there, keep your chin up. This family has been though much, but we'll get through this too."

Julie collected herself and nodded her head. A smile returned to her face, knowing that she would soon see her father again and be able to leave all the bad memories of this place behind. She looked back at her grandparents, and replied, "Thanks for your wisdom and insights, but I really need to let Flint know what's happening. If you'll excuse me, the sooner I get this done, the better."

Victoria gleaned back at her. "There you go dear, that a girl."

Eric felt sorrier for Flint, knowing he was about to receive the old 'Dear John' speech. "Chin up girl – you'll be alright."

Julie felt there was no time like the present, so she left the house to find Flint. She remembered seeing drop cloths spread on the ground near the pond, so she headed off in that direction. Julie took her time as she prepared how she would break the news to Flint. She soon spotted Mike and Flint and walked over to them.

Mike saw her approaching and knew what was coming. He rested his hand on one of Flint's shoulders. "Hey kid,

I've got to take a hell of leak, I'll be back soon."

Flint looked up and shook his head. He then spotted Julie walking towards him. He leaned against the rake and gave her a big smile.

Julie returned his smile, but her expression changed quickly to a more serious one.

A butterfly sensation grew in Flint's stomach, and he instinctively knew that something wasn't right. No kiss or warm embrace was received. Now confused, he asked, "What is it Julie?"

Julie sat cross-legged on the ground and motioned for Flint to sit down next to her. She then began to explain to him the changes soon to come in her life.

Unseen in the distance, Mike was leaning against his rake puffing on one of his *Pall Mall* smokes. Behind his legs appeared Foster, Faye, and Emily. Wearing sullen looks on their faces, they quietly looked on as Julie delivered her parting words to Flint.

A breeze blew Julie's hair in front of her face. She didn't bother to move it away to hide the tears on her face.

Mike and the other three started walking back up the drive to the greenhouse. This was a sad day for all, and it seemed best to just go home and retire for the evening.

After parting with Julie, Flint walked back up the drive-way to his car. The news hit him hard and invoked a great sense of inadequacy within him. Flint couldn't help thinking about what he was unable to offer her. At the same time, he regretted his decision to quit school. These remorseful feelings, combined with all that he and Julie had just gone through together, caused Flint to erupt into tears. Upon reaching his car, he managed to collect his thoughts. He wiped his face, got into the car, and left for home.

The sun was sinking low in the sky, casting a long horizontal ray of light that stretched across the entire east side of the garden. Huddled together beneath the grape vines sat Foster and Faye, quietly taking in the beauty of sunset.

Faye emerged from her trance-like state and faced Foster. "I've given much thought to what you said about not wanting to go back to England, and I feel the same as you do. Instead of returning with the family, I believe it's time for us to join our friends and cross over to the next realm of existence. We've done all we can here, and as much as I will miss this earth and the family, it's time for us to move on."

Foster remained silent for several seconds and took a deep breath. "Yes. I agree. There is much to miss here, and the loss of Sarah still is present in my heart, but we knew this time would come eventually."

Faye leaned her head on Foster's shoulder and gazed ahead. She shed a single tear, and replied, "Yes, yes we did.

They both remained motionless, as the last row of sunlight cast on the garden, finally vanished.

28

I n the weeks that passed, there was plenty of activity at the estate. The moving trucks had packed up and loaded all the family's clothes and furnishings. Now that the travel ban had been lifted, Ethan was able to make plans for the family and the pets to fly back to England. The new owners had also arranged to start bringing in their horses and vehicles.

Despite all that was going on, Mike and Flint continued with the fall clean up. Mike decided he would stick around to see what the new owners were like.

Flint had decided to move back to where he grew up and share an apartment with his old high school buddy, Maxwell. He was starting to accept the way things had to be but realized he couldn't remain working on the estate. Having Julie and the past events as a constant reminder to him was something he didn't care to endure.

In the remaining time spent together, Julie and Flint continued to share some light conversations, along with some laughs reminiscing about Jasper's weird quirks. There wasn't a day that went by that Martin's name didn't come up in conversation. Everyone was still wondering what might have happened to him and if he was alright.

It was a cool Thursday morning at the Woodlands Estate. The family's flight was scheduled to leave the next day. It was agreed by Julie, Flint, Mike, the fairies, and Emily that they would all meet one more time at the gazebo by the pond.

They all gathered that afternoon, but the overall mood was a bit somber. Everyone looked at each other, and then back to the pond. They all were anticipating Martin to suddenly emerge with all his glowing, jovial glory.

Faye jumped up on the windowsill and got everyone's attention. "I want to start by saying that this has been quite a ride. After all, none of us had ever mingled in each other's worlds before all this. If you think it's been strange for you, the same goes for Foster and me. Though we have existed with humankind for a long time now, it's now our decision to move onto the realm that others like us have already gone to. You could say it's a type of heaven for the fairy folk."

Foster stood next to Faye and put his arm around her. He then announced to everyone. "You have all been wonderful, and we will never forget each one of you, and Julie, we will always have a special place in our hearts for your mother and father."

Touched by their words, Julie smiled back. "Thank you both for everything, and all that you have done for me and my family." Julie then addressed everyone else. "I wish we could have all shared more time together."

Mike nodded his head and delivered his feelings. "I know I've been touched by this whole event, and no doubt if I told a psychiatrist what happened he would define me as somebody touched-in-the-head too. But seriously, I've never been so impressed by such an amazing group. Please take no offense, but I'll be glad to have some regular days again." They all laughed, and everyone's mood was raised.

Faye turned to Emily, "Now my dear Foster and I have already discussed this between us, and we want you to join us in our journey to the next realm. You need to move on from this place. Where we are going would suit you well. There are many there who would love to hear your stories from the books and the television movies you've told us about. What do you say, will you join us?"

The whole experience had matured Emily, and she too had realized it was time to leave. She closed her eyes and then opened them widely. "Yes! Of course. That would be wonderful. So, tell me. How do we get there? Are you going to beam us aboard like Scotty from the Star Ship Enterprise?"

Foster blankly stared at her. "Yeah, something like that."

The two fairies then hopped onto Emily's left and right shoulders. Faye blew a kiss, and announced, "We bless you all, but it's time to leave."

A blue light formed around the three of them, followed by a soft crackling noise and they vanished.

Julie wiped some tears from her eyes and turned her attention to Mike and Flint. She moved over to Mike and gave him a big kiss on the cheek. "Thank you for everything, and good luck with the new owners."

Mike winked and smiled back. "Study hard, I'm sure you'll do well in whatever you choose to do with your life." He then left, allowing her and Flint to share their last goodbyes alone.

Flint had to restrain his desire to hold and kiss Julie, and her feeling was mutual. Instead, they agreed the whole adventure was never to be forgotten and promised to write each other. Flint wished her a safe trip and asked her to give her father his best. Julie slowly leaned forward, looked him in the eyes, and kissed his cheek. She then turned and walked away.

Now alone, Flint once again pondered about Martin and

wished he were here to talk to. He surveyed the water for several minutes and reminded himself to be happy about leaving all the long, hot, summer days and hard work behind.

Flint turned to leave when he heard a noise from the pond. He looked back and saw a group of bubbles break the surface. He waited ten seconds, but nothing happened. Flint figured it must have been a large fish feeding near the surface of the water.

The next day, Nadia and Karl dropped by to give the family a heartfelt send off. Flint and Mike shook hands with Eric and Victoria and wished them well. Afterwards, Flint knelt and gave King one more big squeeze. Polly looked extremely miserable in her cat carrier and couldn't wait to leave. Though she was going to miss the place, she just wanted this journey to over soon as possible. As the station wagon exited the driveway, everyone exchanged long goodbye waves.

Mike and Flint talked with Nadia and Karl for a spell and then walked back to the parking lot by the greenhouse.

Mike leaned on Flint's car. "Guess, this is it kid." He offered him a cigarette; but Flint declined.

"Yeah Mike, I can't say it was all that much fun working here, but I will no doubt miss you and your friendship.

It was apparent to Mike that Flint was starting to get a little choked up, so he broke the ice. "Flint, this kind of work never really suited you. Being the sensitive and creative guy you are, I'm sure you'll find your place in the world. Keep your chin up, stay away from that wacky tobacco, and you'll be alright. You'll find another girl, and I guarantee that she won't be the last either. Good luck, kid. I'll miss ya'."

"Me too, Mike. I hope the new tenants don't arrive with

anymore creatures like Jasper."

Mike spit on ground. "Yeah, I hope not. Alright kid, take care of yourself."

Flint drove off with a smile on his face, but there were still some mixed emotions that overcame him as he passed the main house, the bridge, and the gatehouse.

Flint also pined that he and Julie had never made love. However, on reflection, Flint realized that such a union would had made their separation all that more difficult. He drew a heavy sigh and decided to leave it all behind him.

Flint left the entrance and gave the Woodlands Estate one more glance. He wouldn't return for another forty years.

Several weeks passed, and the full moon was high in the midnight sky above the Woodlands Estate. All the lights were off in the main house, and the entire property glowed from the brightness of the moon. From the center of the pond Martin shot up, creating a huge splash. He twirled high above the pond momentarily hoovering in the air and then dove head-first back in the water. Instinctively knowing the family had left, he began his non-stop journey back to England.

Epilogue

Many years had passed at the grounds of the Woodlands Estate, and the lives of the people who once lived and worked there had changed as well.

Eric and Victoria loved Ian's parents' cottage and were glad to have returned to England. They were incredibly happy to be able to share their remaining years living with the Ethan and Julie.

Mike stayed on working for the Australian owners for a few more years and then retired. Despite his cigarette use, Mike lived to a ripe old age, but he never reunited with Flint or any of the other guys.

Marco finished out his tour and was decorated with high honors for his bravery on the battlefield. He was also well-liked by the men under him and always helped his buddies with the loan of a few bucks or some super weed he would obtain. Unfortunately, the day before he was to return home, he went missing in action. His body was never recovered, and it was assumed that he may have been either executed or recruited to a secret military operations team.

Ryan returned home and ended up working full-time for the county. He married, had a daughter, and retired with a full pension. Now living in New York City, he often has a story to tell about some of the colorful characters he worked with – Jasper being one of them.

Nadia and Carl ended up having a large family of five and remained living in Karl's house. Both were now retired and blessed with the support and love of their children. Nadia still wears tight sweaters and tons of perfume.

Julie missed Flint for a spell, and they only exchanged a few letters. Eventually they fell out of contact with each other. She had finished design school and landed a job designing women's clothes for a major clothing manufacturer. After several years, she moved up to a managerial position that involved approving designs from young artists who were just starting out. Julie eventually married. She and her husband still reside in England and have been blessed with a meaningful and prosperous life.

At the Clark residence in England, Ian and Ethan sat playing a board game on the back porch. Both men where now
in their early eighties. Ethan's hair had receded a little,
but he still had a youthful look to his face. Ian still exuded a youthfulness about him as he passionately played
the game.

Several minutes of quiet strategy passed, and Ian looked
up at Ethan. "Ya' know, what we need is some *Captain
Crunch* to push the old noodle into hyperspace. Wada'
you say brother'?"

Ethan liked the idea, and after considering the effects of
the sugar rush, he agreed. "Sure, why not."

Ian joyfully walked into the house, to prepare two heap-
ing bowls of the stuff for them. On his way to the kitchen,
he passed through the living room.

In the living room, on top of the fireplace mantel were
many framed pictures both large and small. Some pictures were of the entire family shown with King and
Polly, and others showed Julie and her husband at different stages of their lives. There was even a picture of the
crew at the Woodlands Estate. The day Ryan and Marco
had left to join the service, Eric had Nadia take a picture
of everyone in front of the main house. All the way to the
left, stood Julie and Flint together with Flint holding his
guitar.

Julie was happy to have this photo because it reminded
her of her first love. Also, if you looked extremely hard
in the brush behind where Flint was standing, you could
see the faint figures of both Faye and Foster holding each
other arm in arm.

To the right of the fireplace mantel was a bookcase with
several more framed photos. There was a picture of Ethan
standing next to tall young man, shaking hands. Below
the pictures were a row of seven hardcover books of various titles.

The author of all these books was Cleveland Douglas. The student that Ethan had much praise and promise for had gone on to become a well-regarded, established author. Two of his books were adapted to the big screen and did quite well. Cleveland later became a college professor and continued the gift of teaching to many new and aspiring writers.

This was the mission that Martin was to assist Ethan in doing. It wasn't about him becoming the president or some famous musician, but rather to ensure that he would carry on the gift of educating young minds. The proud looks on their faces in the photograph was proof that Ethan's task had been accomplished. However, Martin hadn't returned to his home realm yet, for he still had one more mission to accomplish.

At the same time back in New York, the fall brought cool nights and comfortable days to the Hudson Valley. The colored leaves fell on the ground, as Flint plucked his guitar on the porch of a small cabin nestled beneath the Schawangunk mountains. He was now fifty-nine years old. Though he could no longer sport his long hair, the years of hard work and attention to his body left him in rather good shape.

Flint had married twice, and had dabbled in several different work arenas, but he was always devoted to his original music for guitar. His friend, Maxwell, introduced him to the world of sales. Eventually, he landed a job selling musical instruments and found he could sell guitars and play them too. He also performed his repertoire for restaurants, cafes, and private functions. The two combined enabled him to earn a modest living.

His first marriage ended after seven years but several years later, he met a wonderful, talented woman who believed in him. They married and were together for eighteen years until she became ill and died abruptly.

Devastated and alone, Flint was once again floundering with what do with his life. He was still too young for retirement, and his passion for music remained dear to his heart.

Flint stopped playing and put his guitar away. At that moment, a peculiar feeling inspired him to get in his car and go visit the estate he worked so hard on forty years ago.

Strangely, the time flew by, and he arrived at the estate. As he pulled into the driveway, he noticed how much larger the trees and bushes had grown. Now passing the gatehouse, the memories immediately started playing back in his head. He passed the cabin and then slowed the car before approaching the stone bridge. Before crossing the bridge, he decided to park the car and get out.

He was now standing in the middle of the bridge, and the memory of Julie standing soaking wet with tears in her eyes became as real as the day it happened.

Flint closed his eyes and dismissed the vision. He turned around and gazed down the length of the pond. Some of the same trees were still there, but others he remembered were no longer standing.

The property seemed strangely quiet and still. There were no sounds or activity coming from any direction. Flint expected any moment for someone to come and chase him off. After all, it was obvious the property was still being very well cared for.

The gazebo was still standing in the distance, but it showed some signs of age. Seeing it again conjured more past emotions for Flint. The recollection of his union with Julie, combined with the recent loss of his second wife, caused a sinking feeling to overcome him.

Flint stood there for several minutes in silence with his eyes closed. Suddenly, Flint felt his whole-body tingle, and with his eyes now fully opened he was aware of a familiar green glow. To his astonishment, arched halfway out of the water in all his green glory was Martin.

Flint peered back at Martin in quizzical awe, and he excitedly blurted, "Martin! We... I... thought you were gone forever. What happened to you?"

Flint quickly sat on the bank of the pond, and Martin moved closer, and replied, "Well, let's see. After I ejected Julie from Jasper's dimension, the portal immediately closed. We were about to tangle when the elders of his world intervened and reprimanded him. Mind you, as a race they were highly intelligent and a rather friendly lot. They were very accommodating, and I enjoyed their watery Shangri La. It turns out that Jasper was the only worm in the apple, and he was punished for his misdoings. In their dimension, my abilities to move through land, and connect with water were temporarily useless. Unfortunately, the elders weren't unable to send me back until the following full moon. By that time, everyone but Mike had already left the Woodlands Estate."

Flint was thrilled to know that Martin had survived and was once again in his presence. "So, I take it, you returned to England to be with Ethan and his family?"

"But, of course, and it has been a pleasure to have watched Julie grow and become the wonderful woman she is. It was a pity that things didn't work out for the two of you, but it just wasn't meant to be, my lad. Also, my purpose on Earth was fulfilled with Ethan. His specific talents fostered the inspiration of many of this world's young writers, especially one. Ethan's life isn't over yet, but his purpose in this lifetime has been completed."

Flint was quiet for a few seconds, and then he quizzically asked, "Then why are you still here? Why haven't you returned to where you came from?"

Martin rose out of the water a little, and replied, "I have remained here for one purpose only, and that is because I knew one day you would return here and would need my assistance. That day has finally arrived, and I have an important message to tell you before I return."

Martin continued, "Flint my boy, you have grown older, and I can sense you have experienced your share of ups and downs. You have done well, and I am proud of the man you've become."

Once again, a melancholy feeling overcame Flint. Wearing a disparaged look on his face, Flint stared at the ground and explained. "Looking back on my life, I made a bad decision to leave school, and wished I studied to become something more than just a salesman and a want-to-be musician. I just found it exceedingly difficult to devote passion to anything but my music. I've been able to make a meager living with various jobs, but now I find myself at a crossroads.

Martin smiled. "Flint, it makes no difference what you haven't achieved in life. All your life experiences have been your lessons to learn, and you mustn't compare yourself to anyone else in this world. What's more important is who you are inside and how you treat others. I can see you still grow your fingernails a tad longer on one hand, and I sense your music is filled with much beauty and passion. You must continue to share this gift with the world. Don't be so disparaged. You still have some more stops to make along your train of destiny. Believe in yourself, and you will succeed with your passion. There will be another love for you in the future, but you must accept and love yourself first. Remain focused and everything else will fall into place. Bye Jove give it all you've got my good man! I have faith that you can do it."

Martin's body was now half out of the water, and his green aura filled the entire corner of the pond. "My work is done here, and it's time for me to return home. Farewell Flint, it's been an honor to serve you." Martin spiraled up and out of the water and dove headfirst back into the pond. The glow from his aura remained below the surface of the water for a few seconds and then disappeared.

Flint started walking back to his car but was halted by the familiar smell of cigarette smoke in the air. He carefully looked in all directions to see if anybody was around. Several moments passed, yet no one seemed to be anywhere in sight. Flint once again caught the whiff of tobacco in the air and the smell reminded him of Mike and the crew.

Flint began to experience a wave of consecutive memories. He recalled the jokes, the fairies, Marco's air-guitar antics, Ryan's lengthy stories, and all the events he experienced while working on the estate. He pondered that he hadn't experienced that type of connection again in his life and wondered if he would have another experience such as that.

At that very moment, unseen to Flint, the spirit of Mike stood right behind him. Mike could have appeared to Flint and given him some more words of encouragement, but he knew Martin had told him all he needed to know. Mike smiled with the knowing that he would one day see Flint again. He spit on the ground and slowly vanished.

Flint returned to his car, but before starting the engine, he reflected once more on Martin's words and advice. Now with his purpose in life renewed, Flint left the Woodlands Estate forever.

ACKNOWLEDGEMENT

I would like to pay homage to the following giants of fantasy and science fiction writing that helped me to fuel my imagination. Rod Serling, Richard Matheson, Charles Beaumont, H.G. Wells, and Jules Verne.

Thanks to the following people that encouraged me to create this story. Joyce Benedict, Derek Green, Todd Dezago, Sarah Shepard, John Fried, Libby Cozza, Mari Griffin, Darryl Wilbur, and Robert Tompkins.

Also, thanks to the musicians and groups that both directly and indirectly inspired me to create my music. Vladimir Bobri, Segovia, Julian Bream, Simon & Garfunkel, Jimmy Page, Pete Townshend, CSN&Y, The Moody Blues, Jethro Tull, Pink Floyd, Genesis, Yes (Jon Anderson), Gentle Giant, Billy Shears, George Harrison, and Todd Rundgren.

ABOUT THE AUTHOR

Garth Green

A native of the Hudson Valley in upstate N.Y., for the past 40 years he has performed his acoustic guitar repertoire for private functions, cafes, and restaurants. Alongside performing, he has sold guitars in a retail environment. This is his debut fiction story that captures his appreciation for the natural beauty of the area and his affection for the mysteries of the universe.

Made in the USA
Middletown, DE
14 March 2021